PRAIRIE STATE BOOKS

Mr. Dooley in Peace and in War
Finley Peter Dunne

Life in Prairie Land
Eliza W. Farnham

Carl Sandburg
Harry Golden

The Sangamon
Edgar Lee Masters

American Years
Harold Sinclair

The Jungle
Upton Sinclair

Twenty Years at Hull-House
Jane Addams

They Broke the Prairie
Earnest Elmo Calkins

The Illinois
James Gray

The Valley of Shadows:
Sangamon Sketches
Francis Grierson

The Precipice
Elia W. Peattie

Across Spoon River
Edgar Lee Masters

The Rivers of Eros
Cyrus Colter

Summer on the Lakes, in 1843
Margaret Fuller

Black Hawk: An Autobiography
Edited by Donald Jackson

You Know Me Al
Ring W. Lardner

Chicago Poems
Carl Sandburg

Bloody Williamson: A Chapter
in American Lawlessness
Paul M. Angle

City of Discontent
Mark Harris

Wau-Bun: The "Early Day"
in the North-West
Juliette M. Kinzie

Spoon River Anthology
Edgar Lee Masters

Studs Lonigan
James T. Farrell

True Love: A Comedy of the
Affections
Edith Wyatt

Windy McPherson's Son
Sherwood Anderson

So Big
Edna Ferber

The Lemon Jelly Cake
Madeline Babcock Smith

THE LEMON JELLY CAKE

HE LEMON JELLY CAKE

Madeline Babcock Smith

Introduction by Dan Guillory

University of Illinois Press
Urbana and Chicago

Publication of this book was supported by a grant
from Nettie Lou Samuels.

Introduction © 1998 by the Board of Trustees of the University of Illinois
Manufactured in the United States of America

ISBN 0-7394-2561-7

UNIVERSITY OF ILLINOIS PRESS
1325 SOUTH OAK STREET
CHAMPAIGN, ILLINOIS 61820-6903
WWW.PRESS.UILLINOIS.EDU

INTRODUCTION

DAN GUILLORY

On August 4, 1952, the venerable Boston publishing house of Little, Brown and Company brought out *The Lemon Jelly Cake,* a first novel by Madeline Babcock Smith, an unknown sixty-five-year-old grandmother who wrote a poetry column for the Decatur (Ill.) *Review,* operated a small antique shop, and gave lectures on such topics as gardens and antiques. The book enjoyed an immediate and astonishing success. It was named "Book of the Week" by the Associated Press, whose book reviewer pronounced it "delightful," and *Woman's Day* magazine serialized it in three successive issues. *The Lemon Jelly Cake* was recorded as a Talking Book for blind or visually impaired readers, and the United States Information Service selected it for inclusion in embassy libraries.

In the highly literary culture of the early 1950s, nearly every important newspaper and periodical reviewed *The Lemon Jelly Cake,* typically giving it unqualified praise. Jane Cobb, writing in the *New York Times Book Review,* described it as a "sophisticated, even urbane novel." Lisle Bell of the *New York Herald Tribune,* seizing on Smith's central metaphor of the lemon cake, concluded that the book "melts in the mouth." Pamela Taylor of *The Saturday Review* observed that it was an "endearing novel of small-town life in a pre-Freudian era." Helen Schrader of the Chicago *Tribune* acknowledged the popular nature of the novel by calling it "pure corn, but the most delightful corn we've come across in a long time." With notices like these, sales were brisk, and *The Lemon Jelly Cake* was rushed through five printings. But when the author suddenly died on December 15, 1952, just four months after the novel's debut, *The Lemon Jelly Cake* disappeared from the literary scene.

All appearances to the contrary, Madeline Babcock Smith did not spring to life as a fully formed, best-selling author. Although she lacked a national reputation when *The Lemon Jelly Cake* first appeared, she had for some time been laying the groundwork for her career as an author. By the time of her death, she had published several chapbooks of her own poetry as well as short stories in the Chicago *Daily News* and *Capper's Farmer*. She had even published a mystery novel—in serial form, in the Decatur *Review*.

Born on June 11, 1887, in Rochester, Illinois, Madeline Babcock closely resembled her fictional counterpart, eleven-year-old Helene Merriam Bradford. Rochester, now virtually a suburb of Springfield, became the model for the fictional village of Tory. Like Helene,

Madeline was the only child of the village doctor. As if to cement the connection between art and life, the author chose her own mother's maiden name (Merriam) as the middle name for her talkative young heroine.

When Madeline Babcock was nine years old, her family moved to Springfield. She later attended Springfield High School and studied for two years at the relatively new University of Chicago (1906–8). In 1910 she married Sidney B. Smith; the marriage was dissolved in 1924. It is not surprising, then, that the fragile nature of the marital bond is one of the major themes in *The Lemon Jelly Cake,* as suggested by the amorous feelings of Sam Blankenbarger (hardware store owner) and Ferd Fuchre (the barber) for Effie Baldwin (the minister's wife)—and, more important, by the Chicago lawyer Winton Fenton's attentions to Kate Bradford, Helene's mother and Dr. Frank Bradford's spouse.

Madeline and Sidney Smith moved to West Macon Street in the West End neighborhood of Decatur shortly after their marriage, and Madeline became loosely associated with nearby Millikin University, opening her home for informal soirees and enrolling as a "special student" from 1927 to 1936. By all accounts she was a bookish and literary person with a well-cultivated sense of humor and strong ties to the literary set in Springfield, counting the poet Vachel Lindsay among her close personal friends. Further evidence of her literary life appears in her copy of Shakespeare's plays, which is heavily annotated. At her graveside, a Millikin University English professor named Davida McCaslin read Smith's favorite passages from Keats, Browning, and Thomas Wolfe.

The author's inspiration for *The Lemon Jelly Cake* was a hypochondriac neighbor who, like Flossie Blankenbarger, suffered from bizarre ailments, including "palsy of the stomach." A humorous short story based on this neighbor earned Smith a berth at the Breadloaf Writer's Conference in 1950 and, though still in rough form, attracted the attention of Rachel Mackenzie of *The New Yorker*. The piece was ultimately rejected by the magazine, but Smith doggedly began expanding and rewriting it. Eventually, Mackenzie suggested that Smith send the book-length manuscript to various publishers, one of which (Little, Brown) bought it in its unfinished form.

Although Mackenzie continued to suggest editorial changes throughout 1951, the primary editor of the final draft was John Woodburn, one of the most talented editors at Little, Brown. His other clients included Eudora Welty and J. D. Salinger. By the early summer of 1952, the manuscript of *The Lemon Jelly Cake* was essentially complete. Smith, accompanied by her daughter Jane Schroyer, visited Breadloaf briefly and then traveled to Manhattan for the formal launching of the book on August 4, 1952.

The editors at Little, Brown hosted a cocktail party in Smith's honor. She also visited the Algonquin Hotel, that quintessential literary mecca of the 1950s, where she posed for the famous photographer Lottie Jacobi. *The Lemon Jelly Cake* then began its upward sales spiral, with each new printing quickly selling out. But twin tragedies struck: John Woodburn died in October 1952, and by mid-December Smith herself was dead, having been fatally stricken with cancer. Because of various internal changes at Little, Brown—and the vagaries of the publishing world in general—*The Lemon Jelly Cake* slipped into oblivion, even though Paramount Pictures had expressed a strong interest in buying the film rights to the text. Eventually, Smith's three children—Elbert, Emmy Lou, and Jane—allowed the copyright to expire.

Because of its loose, episodic structure, *The Lemon Jelly Cake* is rather difficult to classify. It cannot be neatly pigeonholed because it is part memoir and autobiography, part roman à clef (Helene, Kate, and Frank Bradford being obvious stand-ins for Madeline, her mother Emma, and her doctor-father Oliver)—and even part bildungsroman or "education novel," since Helene resembles a whole line of precocious young narrators, including Pip, Huck Finn, and Holden Caulfield. Like her male counterparts, Helene faithfully records every detail, although her overall interpretation of the facts is often ludicrous. A good example is when she confuses "hoar" and "whore" after she and her best friend, Gracie Baldwin, accidentally visit Miss Lou's bordello in Springfield.

The city of Springfield is just one of the many places beautifully evoked in the pages of *The Lemon Jelly Cake.* Turn-of-the-century Springfield had a big central square where the fashionable elite could see and be seen. It was also the site of Dodd's Drug Store, where chocolate sodas could be had for a nickel (toothpicks and water were free). The Leland Hotel offered bountiful meals and palatial suites for the political mavens who lodged there on business trips. And, of course, there were poignant reminders everywhere of Abraham and Mary Todd Lincoln, as Helene acknowledges: "Herndon's store . . . brought me back to reality for this was a historical spot. Here, Mrs. Lincoln had bought quantities of beautiful dress materials, shawls, and fine laces. She had hoarded these in trunks when she came back to Springfield and lived in a darkened room after her husband died."

An obsession with place has always been a hallmark of Illinois literature, from the virgin prairies of Eliza Farnham and George Flower to the deafening cityscapes of Carl Sandburg and Saul Bellow. But it is the ambience of village life that dramatically engages Madeline Smith's literary imagination. Tory is an archetypal Illinois village, defined by its rich culture centered on food and gossip, a cozy little place where people always seem to be eating and talking. In Tory culture, external appearance counts mightily: no house could be without a gilded rolling pin proudly displayed on the wall, or tall vases overflowing with pampas grass, or ceremonial dinner plates with red ribbons inserted in their edges—or a cast iron deer on the front lawn. The women in Tory are strictly defined by these artifacts and by the culinary specialties they prepare. Kate Bradford is renowned for her lemon jelly cake; one of her neighbors, Antha Jones, is celebrated for her angel food cake and homemade ice cream.

The summer of 1900, when the story occurs, is filled with such foods and household items. On back porches and swaying hammocks and picnic tables, the main characters consume endless servings of cake, ice cream, fried chicken, cookies, doughnuts, and ice tea (cooled with chunks of pure, unpolluted pond ice). If evil exists in Tory, it does so on a small, nonthreatening scale. Physical violence is sublimated into friendly competition for the prize jar of pickles at the state fair. Like the distinctive illustration on the original dust jacket, painted in an American Primitive style reminiscent of both Grandma Moses and Norman Rockwell, Tory is an idyllic setting, "the buckle on the cornbelt." The houses are decorated in Gingerbread Gothic, the elm trees are mathematically straight, the men stand proudly in braces and celluloid collars, and the women are dignified in long gingham dresses. Rooms are filled with antique furniture, creating a "black walnut and golden oak world," and life hums along peacefully at an "even counterpoint."

One of the acute pleasures of reading—and rereading—*The Lemon Jelly Cake* is to observe the subtle stratagems employed by Kate Bradford to subvert this charming but nevertheless stifling world of Tory. She maintains a radically simplified household, thereby freeing herself from onerous chores and providing time for a life of the mind. And she takes daily comfort in her famous—if determinative—hypothesis: "Life is in layers. Everybody is in his own layer and can't get out. I'm in the Tory layer." Struggling to maintain her identity, Kate reveals her frustration near the end of the book when she laments, "Sometimes I wonder if the record of my years will only be written on the labels of glasses of jelly and jams and cans of fruit."

Kate's escape from the humdrum life of "the Tory layer" is precipitated by Winton Fenton, a suave and articulate lawyer from Chicago. He visits the Bradfords repeatedly during the summer of 1900, ostensibly to go fishing with Frank or to deliver presents to Helene. But as is painfully obvious to everyone, Winton is hopelessly smitten with Kate and begins to flirt openly. Like poor Effie Baldwin, the minister's wife who ran off with the barber and spent the night in a tent with him at a Chautauqua on the Illinois River, Kate Bradford succumbs to her admirer's charms. She takes the train alone to Chicago, supposedly to go shopping with Aunt Fan, her friend from Springfield, and the tongues of Tory commence to wagging. Eventually, Kate returns from the bright lights of the big city to the snug familiarity of Tory.

Frank responds to Kate's departure by blaming himself and his time-consuming occupation. Later, he welcomes her back with open arms, and she proceeds to share her revised version of the life-as-layer-cake hypothesis: "No *layer* ever won a prize at the fair. It has to be the whole cake, or nothing at all." If Kate's hasty revision seems facile and implausible, it is partly because of her previous assertions and partly because of the lingering suspicion that fictional art could once again imitate real life. Would Kate, like her creator, ultimately demand a complete and final separation from her husband?

Whatever interpretation—modern or postmodern—that readers place on this ending, it certainly achieves closure. *The Lemon Jelly Cake* has a definite architecture: it begins with a funeral and ends with the return of a prodigal. In between, a number of events occur, including the "unbirthday" party for Helene, the ceremonial releasing of a banded eagle (subsequently shot by one of the locals), and the hospitalization of Canary Cummings, the only African-American character in the text and the beneficiary of the villagers' unusually enlightened sense of social justice. A steady stream of verbal humor informs each episode, as when Antha Jones confuses Napoleon and Caesar in the serious context of a caesarean section. Smith also relies on a virtual encyclopedia of droll names: Barbed-Wire Ernie, Spider Benson, Tater Tayler, Captain January (a cow), and Old Mike (a horse).

The not-so-secret ingredient of *The Lemon Jelly Cake* is a sustaining sense of wonder at the unspoiled beauty of Illinois. William Wordsworth just happened to be Madeline Smith's favorite poet (as evidenced by her heavy annotation of his works), which may explain the charged and poetical quality of Helene's feelings—for example, she parks her brand-new bicycle by her bedside in the evening so that "the handle bars were lacquered with moonlight." Somewhere in our collective imagination there must be a singular place like Tory and a sensibility like that of Helene Bradford: "I looked outside. The sun was shining. A beautiful curtain of morning glories hung on the porch. Inside, Mrs. Antha and Uncle Will were smiling at us. The cookies were rich and crumbly. The new century was starting us on the best of all possible worlds."

No one will argue that *The Lemon Jelly Cake* is a masterpiece or even a major work of fiction. But it is a moving and highly readable minor work that preserves an important moment in the cultural life of Illinois. After forty-five years of unfortunate neglect, it certainly deserves a new printing—and a new generation of readers.

THE LEMON JELLY CAKE

TO
Al, Emmy Lou, and Jane

ONE

We sat around the table in the dining room of our little cottage in Tory. There was my father, Dr. Frank Bradford; my mother, Kate; and I, their only child.

It was early June, 1900. The stoves were down and stored in the woodshed. Tater Tayler, one of Papa's patients, always left his potato patch in the spring and fall to move the stoves in and out. I could never decide which I liked best, the roominess of summer or the coziness of the big base-burners with their isinglass windows.

There was something dear about the house with its old furniture, castoffs from my father's boyhood home. It reflected the black walnut and golden oak world in which we lived but it was without its gloss. If a leading magazine's contention that every lady must have a vase of pampas grass in her parlor were true, then Mama was merely a woman.

"Your mother never has a vase around without flowers in it," my father once told me. "That's part of her philosophy of life. Don't forget that, Helene." That

3

day the small blue glass rose-bowl in the center of the table held a few daisies I had picked in the meadow back of the house.

Papa had a philosophy of life, too. Mama said he had and that he seemed to be studying life in this new century as if he were putting it under the big microscope in his office.

We were having our noon dinner. It would have been considered plumb crazy in Tory, at the turn of the century, to have eaten dinner at suppertime!

It was a special day, a funeral day. Weddings and funerals broke the even counterpoint of life in the village. Many months later, I realized what a very special day this was.

"I've taken out your pallbearer gloves, Frank, and put them on the bed with your black coat," Mama said.

"It's the damnedest thing how they expect me to officiate at every funeral," Papa answered. "They seem to expect me to finish the job after I have killed them off."

"But this is different," Mama said. "Harry Simpson wasn't your patient. He hasn't been in this town for twenty years."

"Is Harry Simpson the corpse?" I asked.

"Corpse is such a fancy word. I just read in the paper about some undertaker calling himself a mortician. Our language is getting too damned fancy, too far away from the good old Anglo-Saxon. Besides," he

4

turned to me, "you're taking an unholy interest in funerals."

"But there isn't much else for the poor child to go to in Tory except weddings and funerals," Mama said.

"And church sociables," I added.

"Sociables is a village word, too," Mama said. "I'd say socials."

"Do they call them socials in Newport?" I asked.

"Where did an eleven-year-old hear about Newport?" Papa demanded.

"Mama and I were looking at the pictures in *Harper's Weekly*," I explained.

"In Newport they call them soirees," Mama said.

"My family's getting too fashionable for me," Papa said. "I guess I'll have to stop the *Weekly* and start taking *The Police Gazette*. Right now, we'd better get into our best bib and tucker and start for the funeral."

My father's funeral outfit was a pair of gray trousers and a black coat. I think he'd been married in these clothes. He also wore a white shirt, wing collar and a white silk four-in-hand with a horseshoe tiepin set in brilliants. Mama hated the tiepin and said it looked like a gambler's. But Papa always said, "You don't know as much about these poor people as I do. They need all the luck they can get."

I thought he looked as elegant as the men paper dolls cut from the Butterick books. The minister was

5

a paper doll, too. These two men were in a class by themselves in the village. Coats and stiff collars were a badge of their profession. It seemed to mean so much to the families to see them dressed that way.

In fact, Papa never went out, even on a night call, without his collar. My bedroom opened off Papa's and Mama's room. I can remember waking in the dark and hearing Papa swear and seeing Mama, standing in her nightgown, holding the oil lamp while he hunted for his collar button.

Papa was a tall, dark, slender man. I thought he was handsome and distinguished in appearance but I never dared say so because I was supposed to look like him. Countless times people said to me, "You have such a pretty mother, but you look just like your father."

Mama was dazzling in her beauty. She, too, was tall but there the resemblance ended. She had blue eyes, curly brown hair with red touches in it. Her features were as perfect as a Gibson girl's. Her skin was like a flower petal, a comparison that occurred to me before I read it in a poem.

Papa was as proud of her as I was. I remember one time we had gone into Springfield to have a family-group picture taken. The photographer had said, "Mrs. Bradford, if you'll move over a little, you'll be improved." "Look here, young man," Papa answered belligerently, "God, Himself, couldn't improve on Mrs. Bradford."

6

Mama always acted oblivious of her beauty. She didn't think about clothes all the time, either, like Mrs. Baldwin, the minister's wife. Mama had a mirror on her marble-topped bureau; she must have known how pretty she was.

Mama, too, had special funeral outfits. Today, she had put on her summer one, a white, much-washed dimity with lace insertion up and down the seams. It was warm and her hair clung in damp ringlets round her face, but she never looked wilted. In her hand she carried her black straw hat with the black feather.

Papa always said it was lucky birds could migrate so that the feather could fly from her summer straw to her winter felt. "Just wait until my ship comes in," he often said. "Then I'll buy Mama the most beautiful clothes in all the world." I liked to imagine the ship coming full sail down our little Sugar Creek, laden with golden ducats. Sugar Creek never boasted of anything but a rowboat but it emptied into the Sangamon River and Lincoln was supposed to have walked its banks, so that made it an enchanted creek. But what Papa really meant about his ship coming in was that some day he would own a fruit farm and make a great deal of money on the side.

Mama stood before the mirror in the hatrack and put the jet pins in her hat and we started. We walked down the plank sidewalks of the village to the church, Mama a few steps ahead, as was her custom.

7

"I think I'll take my hat off when I sing," she said. Mama rarely sang in public but since this was a very special funeral she had agreed.

"Yes do," Papa said, and I added, "You must." We both realized she was prettier without it.

"It's just because I'm a performer," she added.

At the church we all separated. Papa stood with the other pallbearers in the bare little churchyard with its one soft maple tree. Mama went up to the front of the church and sat near the piano with Mrs. Baldwin. Since Mrs. Baldwin was the minister's wife, she sang at all church affairs. She had what Papa called a come-to-Jesus voice which made musicians weep and sinners repent.

I walked up and sat with Gracie Baldwin in the front pew reserved for the minister's family. It was a choice place, right across from the chief mourners, so we could see who cried the most. Its disadvantage was that if we wanted to observe the audience, we had to keep turning our necks to rubber.

Gracie, too, was an only child and just my age. She was blonde and pretty but I didn't mind. Beauty was only skin-deep, wasn't it?

In Tory, people looked up to Papa and Mr. Baldwin. They were the only two men in the village who had much education. The church people and the patients went to them for advice and especially turned to them in time of trouble.

8

Papa never sent out bills. It was the custom among doctors. Papa thought this was right. "When people are sick and in trouble, they certainly don't want to be bothered about money," he would say. Like my father, Mr. Baldwin was willing to accept part of his meager pay in potatoes, corn and freshly-made sausage.

Gracie and I shone in their reflected glory. I was known as Doc's little girl and Gracie was the preacher's daughter. We had many privileges on all of which we imposed. We crowded up behind Gracie's father at the graveside services at funerals. We ate at the first table at all church affairs. We chose our own seats in the schoolroom. Our presents were always the first ones taken off the big Christmas tree at the church. We hoisted the flag at the Fourth of July picnics and, together, we had unveiled the one monument of the village. We had been flower girls in various weddings and, whether or not we were taking part, we were invited. And — we sang duets.

Mama often reminded me that because everybody knew us, we must mind our *p*'s and *q*'s. But we were too busy minding other people's business to pay any attention to this. Today, we were in our element in our front seats, ready to observe everything at this unusual funeral.

"Isn't it nice Papa doesn't have to prepare a sermon?" Gracie asked as soon as I sat down.

I hadn't known Mr. Baldwin wasn't going to give a

9

funeral address but I agreed. Papa always said George Baldwin was the laziest man, that he spent his life lying down in green pastures.

"I can't wait to see the man who came down with the body," Gracie said. "He's from Chicago and he's awful rich. He'd have to be, just coming down for a funeral for somebody he wasn't related to. He's a lawyer and his name is Fenton."

"Mr. Winton Fenton," I contributed.

"Have you seen him? Papa doesn't know where he's been keeping himself. He thought he'd come to the parsonage."

"He must have come in on the one o'clock train. Maybe he just walked around," I said.

"Oh look! Here come the Blankenbargers." Gracie turned around. "Papa says Mr. Blankenbarger is stuck on Mama. They had an awful fight. Cross your heart and hope to die if you ever tell."

"I won't," I agreed. I didn't understand how a married man could be stuck on a married woman. The phrase was only used about grown-up boys and girls in the young people's group. It seemed ominous. I was too frightened to ask questions.

"And here come Mrs. Huddleston and Brother Wilbur." I was anxious to get off the subject of the Baldwin trouble. This brother and sister lived together in a big house on the edge of the village. Brother Wilbur was an inventor and one of Gracie's and my special friends.

10

"Maybe he's going to invent a funeral without a corpse — I mean without anybody being dead."

"Helene Bradford! You're being silly. Mama says you're not as grown-up as I am. But Papa says it's because you live in a dream world like your mother."

I didn't like her frankness but a funeral wasn't any place for a fight so again I changed the subject. "Let's count the people."

It was a favorite game of ours. We always played it in church. Gracie had just said, "Sixty-nine" when Mrs. Baldwin started to play the piano. The corpse was coming! There was a "measured tread" down the aisle. I had read the expression in a book and saved it to think about at funerals.

Papa was the first man on his side of the coffin. He looked unhappy. Both he and Mama hated funerals and, although I loved them, I was just smart enough to realize that this was one of the ways they were nicer — and different from — the rest of the villagers.

There was no family, no mourners. That was one of the reasons this funeral was so unusual. On the casket was just one bunch of flowers, the roses from our garden Mama had sent down to the church that morning. Back of the casket walked a man alone. He was tall and handsome. In a magazine love story he might have been described as having classic features, a rugged jaw and flashing blue eyes. He looked about the same age as Papa and Mama. He must be Mr. Fenton.

11

Gracie's father came in from a side room and took his place in the pulpit. He motioned for the strange man to come up to the platform, but the stranger shook his head and sat down in a front pew across from us.

Mr. Baldwin said a short prayer. It didn't mean anything but you knew it was a prayer by the tone of his voice. Then Mama stood up and sang "Nearer, my God, to Thee." She had taken off her hat with the flying feather. The light from the small panes of colored glass shone on her hair. I thought I had never seen her look so beautiful. She was a married madonna, I decided. I could see Papa beaming at her, too.

Mr. Fenton got up, turned around and faced the audience and started to speak. He said he was there because Harry Simpson, the dead man, should have been his friend and wasn't. He then went on to explain that Harry Simpson had been his letter carrier and had come to his office twice a day for twenty years. But the city was a cold place and full of strangers. You accepted the coldness and didn't go out of your way to become acquainted even with a man you saw as often as he had seen Harry Simpson. After that, he went on to say, he had walked around our village and the people he had met had smiled and nodded at him. He realized we knew the man who gave us our mail and were interested in him for we knew all our neighbors and the people we met each day. He seemed to think this was a fine thing.

12

Gracie and I looked at each other and smiled smugly. There was certainly no one in the village we didn't know!

One day, Mr. Fenton said, he realized a different man was carrying his mail. He inquired and found that Harry Simpson was sick and hadn't been on the route for two weeks. He remembered how faithful and pleasant Harry Simpson had been. He recalled that he had always whistled a quiet little tune.

Somehow, Mr. Fenton made me want to cry. I looked at Mama and she was sitting quietly with her hands folded in her lap. But Mrs. Baldwin was wiping her eyes and Gracie was gulping. Even Mr. Baldwin was sitting up straight in his chair.

Mr. Fenton then explained that he thought of himself as an unsentimental person but the sound of that whistle kept running through his head. He put aside his work, telephoned and found out that Harry Simpson was in a hospital. He left his office and went there. He was too late. Harry Simpson was dead.

At that old Mr. Brown, who didn't hear very well, called out, "Amen."

At the hospital, Mr. Fenton found out that Harry Simpson didn't have any family left. He said the city was a refuge for people who were alone. He then decided to bring Harry Simpson home to Tory.

There was more to the talk. I never saw people pay so much attention.

13

At the cemetery, Papa drew Mama to one side. "I think we'd better ask Mr. Fenton to our house for supper. He can't get out of here until the evening train. The Baldwins are taking care of the undertakers."

"I thought someone might come to our house for supper," Mama answered. "And I've made a lemon jelly cake."

"Good girl," Papa patted her shoulder. "You look like a Mary but you act like a Martha."

"The window made a halo on Mama," I said.

"That's fine," Mama turned to me. "But don't count on my having a halo."

TWO

"DO HAVE SOME MORE OF THE JELLIED VEAL," Mama said to Mr. Fenton as we all sat at the supper table. This was one of Mama's company dishes. When she molded it, she added thin slices of hard-boiled eggs and, for a garnish, served it on a bed of lettuce fresh from the garden. Everything else about the meal was as fancy — the dusting of celery seed on the potato salad, the pink-sprigged Haviland dishes, the thin tumblers, the fringed napkins.

"Brother Wilbur brought the ice down on a wheelbarrow. That's why the meat set," I said.

"This past winter was a good ice winter," Papa said. "It froze four inches on the pond. Mrs. Huddleston, where Wilbur lives, has the ice cut and stored in her icehouse. They have a clean pond there, no bad drainage. We're not afraid to use it even in iced tea."

"Do you have much typhoid down here?" Mr. Fenton asked.

"Too much," Papa answered.

"When I was little, they always put a piece of crystal in my water glass. The crystal came down in the family from my great-grandfather, who was a geologist. I'd stir it around and think I was having ice, too." This was a family joke. I had decided it was easier to tell a story on yourself than have other people laugh at you.

"You don't seem the type to be easily fooled," Mr. Fenton said.

I was greatly pleased for I had made up my mind that Mr. Fenton was a storybook character. Maybe he was a prince in disguise. But who was he going to kiss and awaken? I was too young, and Mama was married, and men didn't kiss each other except in Europe. This wasn't just because he was a guest for we often had strange men for meals, patients from the country, Springfield doctors who came out on consultations, men on school business to see Papa who was on the school board. But there were two very special things about Mr. Fenton: he listened to everything we said, and the tops of his shoes were made of the same material as his suit.

"Brother Wilbur brought the ice on a wheelbarrow," I repeated. I didn't want to drop the subject. "I guess he knew we were going to have company. He just gave it to us, not on the bill or anything," I pursued the subject of ice.

"Helene!" Mother cried.

"The child means that I often get paid in potatoes, apples, sausage —"

16

"Sausage! I haven't had any good country sausage in years," Mr. Fenton interrupted.

"You must come down and see us in the winter," Papa said, "and taste some of Kate's sausage and pancakes."

"I'd like that," Mr. Fenton answered. He looked at Mama. It wasn't a pancake look, either.

"Do rich people have to eat sausage?" I asked.

"Helene!" Mama said. "You're acting simply dreadfully."

"I know I shouldn't speak of money," I said. "But I meant people in Chicago and Saratoga Springs."

"I'm afraid Helene lives in a dream world. She gets her ideas out of magazines and books. Besides, funerals always go to her head. That's all the excuses I'm going to make for you." Papa turned to me.

"More than enough, I would say," Mama said. It was poor Mama who had to keep me from being a spoiled, only child. Just the other day, she told Papa that she sat on me all the time but I was such a resilient pancake I always sprang up again. I knew no other child in Tory would ever be called a resilient pancake. It was wonderful to have the smartest mother in the whole world!

The phone rang. "It's always for me at meal times," Papa said, getting up.

"Helene has been brought up in Tory." Mother turned to Mr. Fenton. "But I try to teach her things."

"The romantic poets," I volunteered.

17

"Isn't she a little young for Byron? I don't know much about little girls."

"Byron was — " I started.

"That will do," Mama stopped me.

"How big is Tory?" Mr. Fenton asked.

"Four hundred people," Mama said.

"Four hundred and fifty-six," I corrected her.

Through this conversation we could hear Papa asking, "How close are the pains coming? Have you given her an enema?"

"This always goes on when we have company." Mama couldn't ignore the telephone conversation any longer.

Papa came back to the table. "It's the Cooper girl," he said. "I'm sorry but I'll have to go."

"She's going to have a baby," I explained.

Papa ignored me. He came over and shook Mr. Fenton's hand. "I'm afraid I won't be back before train time, but I want to thank you for coming here with poor Harry's body. It was a very kind thing for you to do. The town appreciates it."

"I could see that by the number of people who came to the funeral."

"There were sixty-nine, not counting Mr. Fenton, the pallbearers and the corpse — I mean the remains," I put in.

"Remains is a worse word, honey." Papa turned to Mr. Fenton. "Helene and her little friend, Gracie, are

18

the town busybodies. They count everything, including the neighbor's washing on the line. But let me tell you again how good it was of you. You must come down and see us again. I'll take you fishing. You said you liked to fish."

"You can't even stay for dessert?" Mama asked.

"No," Papa said. "I'll let Mr. Fenton have my slice of lemon jelly cake. My wife is famous for it."

"I don't blame your husband for raving over this," Mr. Fenton said when the cake was brought on. "It's a picture."

The cake was high and round, and glistening with white frosting. Between each layer was the lemon jelly, a clear custard, yellow and thick. The cake was pretty, Mama was pretty, her house was pretty. She smiled at me because she knew I loved her lemon jelly cake.

"Mama's cake has four layers, most people's only have three," I said.

"Frank told you she counts everything," Mama explained to Mr. Fenton. "It says on the plate, 'It Is Pleasant To Labor For Those We Love.' The plate was my mother's."

"Do you feel that way?" Mr. Fenton asked.

"Sometimes," Mama said. "Usually I feel life is like a lemon jelly cake."

"Just what do you mean by that, Mrs. Bradford?" Mr. Fenton asked. "Do you mean beautiful and light like this cake?"

"Oh no," Mama answered. "I meant that life is in layers. Everybody is on his own layer and can't get out. I'm in the Tory layer."

"I'd think you were the frosting on the cake. You're pretty enough to be the frosting on anybody's cake. When you stood up in the church this afternoon with the shafts of sunlight striking your hair, I — "

"Didn't Mama look beautiful?" I asked. I was used to hearing people compliment her.

"Oh you two mustn't say things like that to me. I'm an old woman. I'm almost forty," Mama said. "I should blush. They do in poems."

"You like poetry?" Mr. Fenton asked.

"Oh yes," Mama answered. "I've taken correspondence courses in English literature from Chautauqua, New York. Sometimes when I think I'll always be in the Tory layer, which isn't one of the top layers of the cake, I think of that line from Keats 'Bright star, would I were steadfast as thou art.' But I try. I scrub and clean and make pickles and jelly and try to do everything the other women in Tory do, except doing my own washing."

"You weren't used to doing as much hard work before you were married?" Mr. Fenton asked.

"Well — "

"But you do have a certain look, a cherished look, as if people loved you. I imagine lots of men have been in love with you. You see I'm like little Helene, I make personal remarks. But I can. I'll probably never see you again. She's lovely, isn't she?" Mr. Fenton turned to me. I nodded.

"I don't have anybody to say such things to. I haven't any family." Mama looked up as he said it. I suppose she had thought he was married. "I guess the lemon jelly cake has gone to my head," Mr. Fenton went on.

"I'm married. Who'd be in love with me?" Mama looked terribly surprised. "Oh, there is the tramp."

"Mama's own tramp," I added.

"Frank's always teasing me about him," Mama explained. "He comes every fall to see me. He's on his way to Florida, then. In the spring he comes back and brings me sea shells. He has them tied up in a red bandanna handkerchief and fastened on a stick he carries over his shoulder just like the tramps in the pictures."

"Some of the shells have parts in them that look just like babies' teeth. Mama lets me play with them sometimes," I said.

"They are pretty. I have them over on the bamboo stand." Mama pointed to a corner.

"Do you give him pieces of the lemon jelly cake?" Mr. Fenton asked.

"If I happen to have any. He likes jelly sandwiches better than anything. The funniest thing, though, was this spring. The tramp came with the shells. Helene was out playing so just he and I sat out in the kitchen and talked. He always tells me about the white beaches, the blue ocean and the palm trees. He thinks I like nature."

"Don't you?"

"I like people better. But anyway this time we talked and talked. When he left, I remembered I hadn't given him anything to eat. In a few minutes he was back at the door. 'Lady,' he said, 'Can I have a bite to eat? I forgot that.' We both laughed then for he doesn't talk like a tramp any more, the way he did when he first came."

"Do you think he's changed since he knew you?" Mr. Fenton asked.

"No, he was just putting on that tramp talk," Mama said. "Tory is the kind of town where tramps are supposed to talk like tramps, farmers like farmers, and ministers like preachers."

"I think he's a prince in disguise," I said.

"That's Helene's favorite character at present," Mama explained. "But, anyway, after the tramp came and asked for a bite he added, 'I mustn't be careless of my protocol.' I had to ask Frank what it meant."

"What did Frank say?" Mr. Fenton asked.

"He said it meant damn foolishness. I had to look it up in Webster."

"I wouldn't have missed this trip to Tory for anything," Mr. Fenton said. "You've given me a lot to think about. The village is nice, too, as well as you Brad-

22

fords. It's peaceful, pretty — with the big elms down the streets — and quiet."

"But you couldn't like it after Chicago," Mama said. "We all went up there to the World's Columbian Exposition, and it was just fairyland! Mr. McKinley said it was 'the world spread out before us.' But even without the fair, Chicago's so grand."

"But it's unkind to people, indifferent," Mr. Fenton protested. "Witness Harry Simpson."

"I know," Mama agreed. "But not long ago I was walking down the street here and a woman stuck her head out of a window and yelled at me, 'Ha, ha, we hire our washing done.' Was that kind?"

"It was damnable."

"Why that was just what Frank said."

"Papa and I are not going to have Mama bending over a hot washtub," I said.

"She picks up these ideas from Frank," Mama said. "But the people here are kind, most of them, and warm and generous. Many of them are second generation Kentuckians, some came from Tennessee. There is a wonderful couple next door, Antha and Will Jones, and Mrs. Huddleston and her brother Wilbur Newlin, who brought us the ice, the Blankenbargers and lots of others. There's the minister, Mr. Baldwin, Frank enjoys him, and his wife, Effie."

"Was she the little woman with the very high collar who played the piano?" Mr. Fenton asked.

"Yes," Mama nodded. "I know she's dressy, but they have a hard time with all the church people feeling they own them. Now, Mr. Fenton, you can go and look at the sea shells, and Helene and I will clear off the table. Then we will start for the station."

"Can I help?" he asked.

"Oh no, before I was married, my father said he'd boil me in oil if he ever caught me asking my husband to do woman's work. My father's a violent man, not a bit like Frank."

"Grandma was very sweet." I felt I shouldn't let Mr. Fenton have too bad an impression of Mama's family.

"She was a saint," Mama turned and gave me one of her firm looks. "And I don't take after her."

"But your father doesn't live here, does he? He wouldn't see me helping you," Mr. Fenton said.

"I don't know. He's a spiritualist."

"A spiritualist?" Mr. Fenton seemed shocked.

"Yes, he's a spiritualist, a Swedenborgian, an atheist and just lots of things. He isn't *really* any of them. He's a Congregationalist. He has what Frank calls an inquiring mind."

"I'll no doubt be safer looking at the sea shells," Mr. Fenton agreed.

As we walked down the shaded street to the station, Mr. Fenton said again, "I do like Tory."

"It's full of the salt of the earth, Papa says so," I

felt called upon to answer as Mama was silent. "When Gracie and I were little, we used to taste the earth to see if it were really salt. But Reverend Baldwin says he meant good people."

"Mr. Baldwin, not Reverend Baldwin. But that's what the child hears," Mama looked up at Mr. Fenton. "We're Doc Bradford and Mrs. Doc Bradford. And they'll speak of you as Lawyer Fenton."

"And I'm Doc's little girl."

"And you don't want Helene always to be in the Tory layer of the lemon jelly cake?" Mr. Fenton asked.

"Oh no, Mr. Fenton," Mama said. "But what am I saying? Everyone is so good to us."

"You might call me Winton or Wint. I've been calling your husband Frank."

"I'll call you Uncle Wint," I said.

"I'd be flattered. If you do I'll bring you a present when I come down again. Your father has asked me to come down and go fishing."

"But we only have catfish down here." Mama's voice sounded almost frightened. She usually didn't mind having company.

"You can bring me a party," I said.

"Helene! The idea of your telling Mr. Fenton — I mean Winton — what to bring."

"What does the child mean by a party?" Mr. Fenton asked.

"I mean paper hats, they pop when you take them

out, and nut cups. It tells about them in *The Youth's Companion.*"

Just then the train came roaring in. A great cloud of smoke enveloped us. The baggage master came out bringing a sack of mail. The undertaker and his helper, who had been staying with the minister, came out from the little depot. People from Tory didn't use the evening train often. There were no other passengers.

"Good-by," Mr. Fenton said. He leaned down and kissed me. "And this is for the frosting of the lemon jelly cake." He leaned over and kissed Mama on the cheek.

"Oh dear!" she cried. I was surprised, too.

"But I might never see you again." He turned and hurried up the steps of the coach.

"My party?" I called after him.

"He didn't hear you," Mama said when he didn't answer.

Mr. Fenton stood on the back platform and waved. The train started. It puffed by the crossing, then it went down the tracks shining in the last rays of the sun. Straight, straight it would go into the very heart of Springfield, Illinois, the capital city, the magic city!

"Was that a frosting kiss Mr. Fenton gave you?" I asked.

"It certainly was only that," Mama answered.

"Do people do things like that in Chicago?" The outside world fascinated me.

26

"I'm sure they do," Mama answered. "I've been reading some plays lately. They are always kissing each other, lightly, and saying *darling*, and they always say *ah* instead of *oh*."

"Papa asks people to say *ah* so he can look down their throats," I said.

"But this is a different kind of *ah*," Mama said.

"*Ah, ah*," I said, quickening my steps to keep up with my mother. I thought I'd better practice sounding stylish, in case Mr. Fenton came back. I hoped he would.

THREE

It was later in June, and hot. Mama had come from a cooler climate and she never became used to the fever of Tory in June, July, and August.

Each evening we pumped water from the well and carried it to the sweet peas. These were Mama's pride and she wanted to keep them going. She always raised just one variety, the pink and white Blanche Ferry Spencer. She sent away for the seeds, which was considered highfalutin of her as everybody else bought theirs, mixed, at the hardware store.

One of my duties was to pick the sweet peas and the nasturtiums. I also was allowed to arrange them. This was supposed to help me become *artistic,* a favorite word of Mama's. Besides, as she explained, every *lady* should know how to arrange flowers beautifully. She had another tenet, learned from her own mother, which was that only a lady could dust. Grandmother's hired girl never saw the dust on the china arbors of her Staffordshire figures.

As I snipped at the sweet peas with the kitchen shears, I decided that their hooded faces looked like

28

nuns, nuns who were dressed up and ready to go to
a fancy ball. I had seen a few nuns on the streets of
Springfield and the medievalness of their habits both
frightened and fascinated me. Papa loved nuns. He said
they made such perfect nurses because they didn't want
to get married. I didn't want to get married, either, but
I hated slop jars. I'd seen enough of illness to connect
them with nursing.

The nasturtiums were different. They scrambled
around on the ground; they were varicolored and vivid
and looked mischievous. Mischievous was a new and
favorite word of mine. It was often used in *The Youth's
Companion.* Papa considered it a silly word but I still
loved it.

I put the sweet peas in a vase made of glass, white
and opaque as milk. Mama let me get out the amber
finger bowl for the nasturtiums. She had a set of these
made of different colored crackled glass. They had
been given to her by her friend in Springfield, Aunt
Fan, whose husband had inherited the rolling mills.
When we were alone and the shades drawn, we often
used the finger bowls after supper. Tory would never
have recovered if they had caught us at this rite.

Right now, I was standing by the front gate waiting
for Gracie Baldwin to come down and play. But it was
Mr. Baldwin who appeared. He was almost running as
he passed by on the other side of the street without
even looking over. Something was wrong! Mr. Baldwin

never hurried, even when he was praying at the end of a sermon and must have known the Sunday roast was drying up.

In a few minutes, Gracie came on the run. "Get your hat! We've got to go to Springfield. They're *living in sin!* We've got to help! It's terrible!"

"Mischievous?" I was still thinking of the nasturtiums.

"Don't stop to talk. Just tell your mother we're going in with Papa," Gracie said.

I ran into the house. Mama was sitting by the window embroidering. Mama was quick with her housework and could usually finish her tasks in time to embroider in the morning. This annoyed the neighbors. Right now she was trying to get the new curtains done before Mr. Fenton came down for his fishing trip. Papa had written him and set the date. Mama had seemed strangely timid about inviting him. I knew it wasn't because she was ashamed of our house or Tory. She never was.

"I'm going to Springfield. On the train! With Gracie and Mr. Baldwin," I called from the front door as I took my little round hat off the hatrack.

"What?" Mama cried.

"It's important!" I called back. "They're living in sin!"

"I don't understand a word you're saying," Mama said. She started to get up. Her embroidery hoop rolled on the floor. She tripped on it. I slammed the door and ran.

30

That evening I heard her explain to Papa that she had decided that if Mr. Baldwin were along it would be all right. She had caught the words, living in sin, but she decided they didn't mean Effie Baldwin or they wouldn't be dragging me along. So she had settled down to her embroidery thinking that Mr. Baldwin must be going in town to preach a sermon on sin, and only worrying because I had on my faded blue gingham.

We had just reached the station when the train appeared around the bend.

"We'll hide behind the building until Papa gets on. Just as it leaves, we'll jump on the back platform," Gracie whispered.

"Is it going to be all right?" I asked.

"Oh, yes! We've got to go. You always help me out. We've got to help Papa. He was just screaming, 'Gosh blame, if this gets out that I'm so careless, I'm ruined. Gosh blame! Gosh blame!'" Gracie's eyes were round with excitement. "You know what that means?"

I nodded in agreement. Gosh blame was Mr. Baldwin's very worst expression. It corresponded to Papa's damn it to hell, while his dad burn was like Papa's damn or hell and his consarn it wasn't any worse than Papa's casual by Jesus. It showed the difference between being a minister and a doctor. If Mr. Baldwin gosh blamed, it *was* serious. I had asked Papa what Mr.

31

Fenton said when he swore, and he said Mr. Fenton would no doubt say "Twenty-three hundred skiddoo," because he was a hundred times more elegant than the people who said twenty-three skiddoo.

We peeked out and saw Gracie's father get on the train. Other passengers went up the steps, and finally the conductor. Then, just as the engine was beginning to puff, we ran and climbed on the steps.

"Let's sit down on the back seat," Gracie said. "I'll tell you all about it before Papa sees us."

"What is it?" I asked.

"It's all just happened. A couple came to our house to get married this morning. They were just getting ready to stand up before Papa and get married when the girl said, 'Which way do the boards run in the floor? You have to stand the way they run. It's unlucky if you stand the wrong way on the boards.'

"Mama was there for a witness and she ran over next door for Mrs. Sturgis for the other witness. They looked like a good five-dollar couple. You know Mama always gets all the money they take in at weddings for her very own?"

I did. It was the only reason I wished Papa were a minister. He would have loved having such easy money, to give to Mama.

"Then Mama said, 'Gracie, run down cellar to see about the boards.' The boards run north and south. They got married after I told them that, and they did

32

give Papa five dollars. They had a horse and buggy and we all went out on the porch and waved at them and said, 'Good luck, good wishes,' and Mama picked a rose off the bush and threw it at the bride. Papa took the paper the man had given him to write it up in his record book, when all of a sudden he began saying 'Gosh blame' and all that stuff I told you. 'They aren't married at all,' he yelled at Mama. 'This isn't an Illinois license. They'll be living in sin if I can't stop them.' 'But how will you stop them?' Mama asked. 'I'll go into Springfield and try to head them off. They told me they were going to drive into Springfield.' 'But how will you find them in that big town?' Mama asked. 'I'll borrow a horse and go out to the Tory road and try to head them off. At least I'll have to try.' He started then for the train. I waited a minute and then I came after you."

"But how can we help?" I asked Gracie.

"I know them. Didn't I go down and look at the boards in the cellar for them? And they never gave me a thing. I thought you and I could spend the day looking for them. They'll probably drive around the Square, everybody does, and we can ask people if they've seen them. Maybe we'd better go up now and tell Papa we're here. He's got a pass, but he'll have to pay our fare."

"Well, dad burn, how did you get here?" Mr. Baldwin said when he saw Gracie and me. He still was in a bad humor.

"We came to help," Gracie said. "I know what those people look like and I can help find them." She explained her theory about going around the Square.

"This is the silliest thing you little girls have ever done and you've done plenty. But I can't throw you off the train. There's nothing for me to do but take you along. Go and sit down in another seat and don't bother me any more. I'm thinking."

"Do you suppose he's thinking about a sermon?" I asked. This was a test question. Papa said George Baldwin got his sermons out of a barrel. I pictured the barrel coming to Mr. Baldwin by express, direct from God. If he were thinking and could make up sermons out of his head, I wanted to tell Papa.

Springfield was the first stop. The B. and O. train pulled into the station. We all got off. Mr. Baldwin reached down in his pocket and handed each of us a nickel.

"I've got to hurry down to the Methodist parsonage and borrow a horse and buggy. I can go faster alone," he said. "You little girls can walk around the Square and look in the store windows. Then you can go down to Dodd's Drug Store and get yourselves each a chocolate soda with the nickels. I'll meet you here around noon at the station. But, here, Gracie," he handed her a quarter. "If I shouldn't be here by then, you can get ham sandwiches at the counter, and pieces of pie and spend the rest for candy. Then don't stir out of the station. I want to get the early afternoon train back to Tory. Now don't talk to strangers when you're in the station. Just sit with each other and keep quiet. Stations are bad places."

We walked down the three blocks to the Square. This was the tough part of Springfield. The street was lined with saloons on both sides. They all had swinging doors, some made of screening with bright pictures painted on them. One had a beautiful scene, a bright blue background on which were a brighter blue waterfall, green trees, and an orange sun. On another was a picture of a lake with a rowboat.

"Do you suppose they put those pictures on the doors to make people thirsty?" Gracie asked.

"Gracie Baldwin! You're not thinking of the ice cream soda when we have work to do?" I asked.

"I guess not," Gracie answered.

A man came out of a saloon door. "He's drunk," Gracie whispered.

"He isn't reeling," I said.

"But he'd have to be drunk," Gracie insisted. "These places are dens of iniquity. Remember the temperance book?"

"Yes," I admitted. This was one of our favorite books. We often took it out from Mr. Baldwin's bookcase and studied it when no one else was around. "I bet his stomach looks just like the pictures of the drunkard's stomach. You know, all bright like a sunset."

35

"Yes," Gracie agreed. "It's awful."

We came to the north side of the Square. The Square! How we both loved it! In the center was the courthouse, the building where Abraham Lincoln had practiced law.

The courthouse, surrounded by a lawn, occupied a block. Around this were the main stores of the town and the banks. It was hard to know which way to turn for there was so much to see. We started our tour at the drugstore with its jars of leeches in the window, paused at the shining, new bicycle shop. Near that was the hardware store, even bigger than Mr. Blankenbarger's. Then there were stores where there were nothing but hats, and stores where there were nothing but shoes. In the general store of Tory, shoes and hats were mixed with groceries and red handkerchiefs. We pressed our noses against the window of the candy store, gazing at the jars of stick candy and the glass trays of chocolates and pink peppermints. It was such fun, just being in Springfield and seeing things. The Square was like fairyland. I wouldn't have been surprised to see a window display of gauze wings, tiny glass slippers and wands tipped with dewdrops.

Herndon's store, on one corner, brought me back to reality for this was a historical spot. Here, Mrs. Lincoln had bought quantities of beautiful dress materials, shawls, and fine laces. She had hoarded these in trunks when she came back to Springfield and lived in a dark-

36

ened room after her husband died. Just last week, Papa
and Mama had been discussing her. Papa had said,
"Poor thing. No wonder. Losing a husband like Mr.
Lincoln would affect any woman's mind." Then Mama
had said, "I'd rather be married to you," and Papa had
answered, "Don't be sacrilegious."

"Let's walk over to Bressmer's," Gracie suggested.
"Their windows are always beautiful."

"But, Gracie," I protested. "We mustn't keep looking
in windows. We'll miss the man and woman who are
living in sin."

"I'm watching," Gracie said.

After we had circled the Square, we walked over to
the courthouse grounds and sat down on a bench. Nothing happened. No couple appeared.

"Shall we go and get our soda now?" Gracie asked.

"Oh, no, we came here to find the bride and groom.
We must do it," I said. "Why do you suppose they don't
show up? You'd think they'd want to drive around the
Square."

"Maybe they've stopped in someplace."

"Where would they stop?" I asked.

"I don't know. Where would people stop who are
living in sin? Papa's so mad at them he's sure they
know they're living in sin," Gracie said.

I wondered what Mr. Fenton — Uncle Winton —
would do if he were trying to find people who were
living in sin. He was a lawyer and so smart — Mama

37

said so. He could find anybody. "We could ask," I suggested.

An older man came along. He wasn't very clean, but he looked friendly. He paused near us.

"We could ask him," I whispered.

"You ask," Gracie gave me a nudge.

"No, you. You're prettier, and besides, this is really your thing. It's your father who started all this."

"Excuse me," Gracie said to the man, "but could you tell me where people would be who are living in sin?"

"Why look here! What do you want to know for?" the man asked.

"It's very important," I said.

"Then I'll tell you. You go down there a few blocks and you'll come to a house. It says *Miss Lou*, painted on the transom. There are some other houses and they've got other names, but I think Miss Lou's is the best. You can tell her Jack sent you."

"See? He *did* know," I said. "We'd better start."

We went down the street where the man had pointed. Gracie and I had never been on it before. It wasn't a nice street, we decided, for it, too, had saloons, although there were also a paint store, men's clothing stores and an implement store. There only seemed to be men on the street.

Then we came to a block where the houses had names painted over the doors, just as the man had said. We passed one called *Miss Sadie* and another one which said *Miss Lily*.

"There's Miss Lou's across the street. I guess they must be places like hotels or boardinghouses. Mama says this town is full of boardinghouses," I said.

We went up the rickety front porch and pulled the doorbell. A colored woman in a spotted dress answered the door.

"Is Miss Lou here?" I asked.

"What do you little girls want? If it's selling something, Miss Lou don't want none of it. You'd better get out," the woman said.

"What's that?" A large woman in a black satin dress with a beaded jet yoke came into the hall. "Come on in. Now what do you want?"

I looked at Gracie. Gracie just stood there. "We — " I hesitated — "We're looking for some people who are living in sin. A man sent us."

"What's that?" the woman asked.

"Are you Miss Lou?" I asked.

"Some folks call me that. But now, what do you want? Is this some church thing? If it is, it's a low-livered thing for them to send little girls here. Go home and tell those praying-sisters I said so."

"A man sent us — Jack." Gracie finally found her voice.

"Her father is a minister." I pointed to Gracie. "But the church didn't send us. You tell, Gracie."

"I don't want to." Gracie was shaking now.

"Agnes, oh Agnes," the woman called. "You come down here. You've had a kid. See if you can make out what this is about, anyhow."

A girl in a dirty pink silk wrapper with lace around the yoke came down the stairs. Several other girls dressed in bright-colored flowing wrappers followed her. They had pink cheeks like dolls and most of them had blonde hair, bright blonde like real gold.

"What is it, honey?" the girl named Agnes asked.

"It's all about a wedding," I said. "Only it wasn't a real wedding and Gracie's papa says they are living in sin. You tell 'em."

"Come here." Agnes motioned to Gracie to sit down beside her on the little settee covered in green plush. I perched on the piano stool which was covered with a fringed red satin throw.

Gracie told the story, all about the wedding and how we had come in on the train.

"But how did you find us?" Agnes said, patting Gracie's hand.

"We asked a man on the street and he told us if we wanted to find anybody who was living in sin to just come here. I think he was joking."

"If that don't beat the band," the older woman said. "Some folks think they're too smart for anybody's good."

40

"The poor little things." Agnes started to cry. This made Gracie cry, too.

"Stop bawling, Agnes," the woman said.

"Do all you people live here?" I asked. It all seemed so strange.

"Oh no, we're just friends who happened to drop in for a call," one of the girls said.

"And now you little girls must run along. We don't know anybody that's living in sin," the older woman said.

At that a girl in an orange wrapper with bright red hair began to giggle. The woman looked at her and she stopped.

"Let me get them something, please," Agnes said. She ran up the stairs and came down with two strands of beads. "Here. I want you each to have a present. A gentleman friend gave them to me. If my little girl had of lived I'd want her to have them. Here," she pointed to Gracie, "you can have the blue ones. They go with your pretty blue eyes. And you," she handed the other strand to me, "you can have these pretty bright red ones. They'll be nice on you because you're dark."

"Oh, thank you! Thank you!" we both cried.

"Now I'll take you to the door," the older woman said. "If there's nobody coming down the street, you can go."

"That was funny," I said when we were outside.

41

"She didn't want people to see us. Do you suppose she was really hiding the people who were living in sin?"

"I guess not," Gracie said. "I don't see the horse and buggy tied down the street. We should have thought about that before we went in."

"They could have left the horse at the livery stable," I suggested. "Did you think there was something funny about that place?"

"Yes. It wasn't a bit like anything I ever saw in Tory," Gracie agreed.

As we neared the end of the block, we saw Mr. Blankenbarger. He was coming out of a house which had the name *Miss Dolly* painted over the door.

"Why, Gracie Baldwin and Helene Bradford! What are you doing down here?" he asked.

"We're helping Papa find someone," Gracie said.

"Your father didn't send you down here?" Mr. Blankenbarger was visibly shocked.

"Oh, no," I said. "We thought it up ourselves." Together we told him the story.

"Well, what do you know?" Mr. Blankenbarger said. "I guess it turned out all right. But you mustn't ever come down here again."

"Oh, we won't," Gracie promised.

"I'm here on business, the hardware business," Mr. Blankenbarger explained as we walked along. "But — but — well you know how it is in Tory. I guess folks would think I ought to stay home and tend to the store, so — "

"So you don't want us to tell that you were doing business in Springfield?" I said.

"You've got the point. I always did say Doc's little girl was pretty smart."

"Oh, I don't know," I said modestly.

"We didn't see you on the train," Gracie said.

"No, I drove out to the Anthony place where they are doing some building and as that is about halfway to town, I decided I'd drive in the rest of the way and — well, take care of some business, like I said. But I tell you what, suppose I take you little girls down to Dodd's drugstore and get you each an ice cream soda, since we don't have a soda fountain in Tory."

"Why, that was where we were going!" Gracie said.

"We have our own nickels for the soda," I said. "We can pay — " Gracie gave me a punch.

"No, this is going to be my treat," Mr. Blankenbarger insisted.

"He's awfully rich," Gracie whispered as we walked through the door.

We sat up on stools at the counter. In shining metal containers over the counter were the syrups — chocolate, pineapple, strawberry, nectar, raspberry, cherry. At the end was one labeled *Don't care*.

"Some day I'm going to take a *Don't care*," I said.

"Oh, you wouldn't dare!" Gracie said.

"Oh yes, I would." I think this particularly fascinated me for Mama would never let me say "don't care" when anyone offered me anything. I had to say definitely either yes or no.

"Well, folks, what'll it be?" the man at the counter asked.

"Chocolate," Gracie said.

"Chocolate," Mr. Blankenbarger repeated.

"Chocolate," I finally said. This was too big a day to take a plunge into the unknown.

The man brought the drinks. They were in tall glasses, each placed in a silver holder with a handle. There was a long silver spoon for stirring, and supping. We lingered deliciously over this drink of the gods, even if it wasn't labeled nectar.

"We must go now and meet Papa at the railroad station," Gracie said when we had finished.

At the station, Mr. Baldwin was walking up and down the platform. "Where have you been?" he asked. "I looked all around the Square for you."

"Did you find the bride and groom?" Gracie asked.

"Yes, I caught them, married them again, too. The young man got another license, an Illinois license. I did it down at the courthouse."

"Did you get more money?" Gracie asked.

"Of course not," Mr. Baldwin answered. "But where have you been?"

44

"We asked where we could find people who were living in sin," I said. "And went there."

"Tell me exactly what you did." Mr. Baldwin seemed excited.

We told him about our visit to Miss Lou's.

"Gosh blame!" he cried. "A whorehouse! Gosh blame!"

"What's that?" Gracie asked.

"Nothing. And old Blankenbarger down there! Never speak of this to *anybody!*" he cautioned us.

I frowned. This was one of my first problems in ethics. My minister was saying not to tell anybody. And yet you always confessed everything to your father and mother. If God had said not to speak of it, I wouldn't, but Mr. Baldwin was just a cross man in a shiny, black alpaca coat. Besides, Papa was smarter than Mr. Baldwin. He could always explain everything.

"Have you had your dinner?" Mr. Baldwin asked.

"No," Gracie said.

"You can take the quarter and spend it," he said. "I had dinner at the parsonage when I returned the rig."

We walked over and sat on the stools at the counter. There were large ham sandwiches under a big glass bell, pies with round, screened fly covers over them, and doughnuts under another bell.

"You pick it out," I whispered. "It's your money."

"We can each get a ham sandwich, that will be ten cents, and each of us a piece of pie. That'll be another dime."

45

"And look," I pointed to a sign. "Doughnuts are two for a nickel."

"And we throw in the water and the toothpicks," the man behind the counter said.

When we were on the train, we sat again in the back of the coach, as far away from Mr. Baldwin as we could get. We knew he was still in a gosh-blaming mood.

"I know what hoar is," I said, after the train started. "It's in Mama's kind of poetry. It's a real thick frost, hoarfrost."

"But it seemed hot in that house," Gracie said.

"I know," I agreed. "But that's what it means, all right."

"We'll have to tell about the beads," Gracie said. We each took our strands out of pockets in the skirts of our gingham dresses and looked at them. How beautiful they were!

That evening, I was sitting by myself in the hammock under the elm trees in our yard. I had been thinking about the flowers I had picked that morning. The women I had seen at Miss Lou's were pretty but they weren't beautiful and fragile like the sweet peas. They were dressed up, but still they didn't look like nuns going to a fancy-dress ball. They were more like nasturtiums. Maybe they were even worse than mischievous, because Papa had said, "Damn it to hell," when he had heard about them. Mama had cried and called me her innocent little lamb. And this wasn't a bit like Mama. I had realized it wasn't the time to press for an explanation.

Then, Gracie came through the gate. I moved over in the hammock to make a place for her.

"Did you get one-two-three from your folks?" Gracie asked.

"Yes," I answered.

"What did your folks do with the beads?" Gracie asked.

"Mama took mine away and threw them in the cook stove and burned them. She said they were dirty and trashy."

"Mama took mine, too," Gracie said. "She boiled them on the stove. She's going to wear them with her light blue silk dress. And they were so pretty — and mine."

"Aren't parents funny?" I said. "My father's a doctor. *We* should have boiled and sterilized the beads."

"We'll never know anybody funnier than our own folks." Gracie shoved on the ground with her foot. The hammock began to swing.

"Never," I agreed. "Mama cried when she heard where we'd been. Then she said, 'But those poor women don't know any better.' I guess she meant the women in the hoarfrost house."

The ropes of the hammock creaked as they swung

back and forth. "You know what," I added, "sometimes I think I don't want to get big and have to understand things."

"You want to get big and marry a rich man like Mr. Fenton, don't you?" Gracie asked.

FOUR

MR. FENTON WAS COMING DOWN THE END OF the week and he was bringing my party. It was the second week in July, not quite a month since he had been down for the funeral, but it seemed like ages. In the meantime, he had written to Mama three times. She didn't show them to me but she did say they were lemon-jelly-cake letters rather than bread-and-butter letters. I had watched her trying to answer them. Once she had torn the letter she was writing into little pieces. It wasn't like Mama.

The party was to be Friday evening. On Monday, Mama suggested we work in the garden since it was hot in the kitchen. The house was flimsy and didn't keep out the heat waves of summer or the prairie winds of winter. It had formerly been a saloon called the *Lone Star.* Prohibition had hit Tory at one time and this one saloon was abolished. Then, as Papa was planning to be married soon, he had bought the building, moved it to its present site and remodeled it. The roof on the back had been raised and there were two small rooms upstairs, but we still called it a cottage. It had been painted white several times but the lone star, which had originally been painted over the doorway, still showed. Being born in a saloon embarrassed me. But Mama said she cherished it like she did the china trinket box with a bicycle girl on the lid which stood on the stand table. The box was a present Mr. Fenton sent to Mama.

This day, Mama and I were tying up the tomato vines on stakes. We used long strips of rags, the same width Mama used for putting up my hair when, on state occasions, she wanted to turn my braids into curls. I hated the process. As we worked, I felt sorry for the tomato vines.

"Kate! Kate!" Mrs. Antha Jones called from next door. "Come on over! I've got egg yolks for you."

"We'd better go," Mama said. "Time, tide, and tomatoes have to wait for Antha."

I understood what was meant by the offer of egg yolks. When Mama was first married, she had been in the Jones kitchen when Antha had just finished beating up sixteen egg whites for an angel food cake. She then took the yolks of the eggs and dumped them in the garbage pail.

"Oh don't do that," Mama had cried. She was frugal both by nature and circumstance.

"Can't use 'em," Antha had answered.

"Well, Frank and I could use them," Mama had said.

Through the years it had taxed her ingenuity to use up these yolks, for Antha was always whipping up angel foods. Mama made jars of salad dressing and all varieties of yellow cake and custards, not to mention a supper dish called Jones's Egg Supreme, for which the yellows were boiled, mixed with cream sauce and served on toast.

"When Jones's Egg Supreme blossoms on our table it means Antha is on the warpath again," Papa usually commented.

Antha was a famous cook but angel food cake was her prize. She made it for all the church socials where, to her delight, it stood a good two inches higher than Minnie Overstreet's. She had won prizes with it at fairs. She made it for weddings and birthday parties and carried it to the houses of mourning. Sometimes she just stirred one together to cheer herself up, as some women buy a new hat. Often, she made one just for our family. She would come over bringing practically a whole cake on the gold-banded chop plate from which it was always served. "Just got hungry for angel food," she would explain. "Now you folks have got to help Will and I eat it up." This was her way of being tactful. It wasn't in her code to present us with a whole cake unless it was for a special occasion. She might make angel foods to show off, as she was often accused of, but when she made one for our family it was from pure goodness of heart.

Antha and her husband Will lived in a big brick house. There was a high Osage hedge between their house and ours. They had cut an opening in this which they called Helene's gate, and I used it often. The Joneses had no children of their own and I was their pet. I was boasting about this at one time, and Mama corrected me. "Well, she is," Antha said. "And there's no use mincing any bones about it."

I loved both Mrs. Antha and Uncle Will. I was invited over to their house for a meal whenever they had anything they thought I would especially enjoy. On cold winter mornings before I was in school when Mrs. Antha was frying hot doughnuts for breakfast, Uncle Will would come after me. He'd bring a shawl along and carry me, clad in bathrobe and crocheted bedroom slippers, through the snow. He never went to Springfield without bringing me a present. In the R months, this was often a paper bucketful of oysters. The Joneses didn't like oysters. Mrs. Antha called them nasty, slippery things. But this didn't keep them from going to the oyster suppers at the church. "We fill up on the stew part, and the pickles and crackers," Antha always explained.

Mama and I walked through the cut in the hedge, entered the kitchen on tiptoe. It would have been a sin to jar an angel food cake while it was baking.

"You don't have to walk like that, the cake's baking in the summer kitchen," Antha said.

"I always forget you have two ranges," Mama answered.

"Take the rocker, Kate." Antha pointed to the chair with its patchwork cushion. I sat down on the footstool.

The kitchen was Mama's favorite room at the Joneses'. As they said in Tory, the floor was so clean you could eat off it, you could see your face in the polish of the stove, and get your eyes put out by the sparkle of the copper utensils. A red and white checked tablecloth covered the table in one corner. This was where we ate when I was the only company. Mrs. Antha was a lover of calendar art and several hung on the wall, as well as a calendar plate from a Springfield grocery store. When I had told her Mama burned up our calendars, she had pronounced her notional.

"Mr. Fenton would like this kitchen," Mama said. She and Mrs. Antha had evidently discussed him before. "It's what he thinks all Tory is like — honest, and friendly, and warm; I don't mean warm like summer with this nice breeze coming in."

"I've been thinking I ought to tell you something." I saw Mama wince and I didn't like conversations that started this way, either. Mrs. Antha then pointed to a clock which stood on a shelf. "I put the secrets about how I make my angel food in the clock. If anything should happen to Will and I, I want you, Kate, to take out the paper and destroy it. I don't mind if you read it first. But I don't want it to ever fall into the hands of Minnie Overstreet."

Minnie was Antha's avowed enemy, but in many ways they were alike. Minnie lived in a brick house as big as Antha's. They both had inherited farms from their fathers. They were both famous cooks and housekeepers. Antha was of more ample proportions but they both had a determined look. They were older women than Mama, but neither one had any children. Minnie's husband had been dead for five years. Antha said he died from Minnie's meanness, but Papa called it pneumonia.

Mama already had Minnie's recipe for her specialty, an elaborate fruit cake. Mama had never made it because she said you had to own a section of land before you could afford such a luxury. On the bottom of the paper, on which it was written, were the words, "Don't give this recipe to anybody and never give it to Antha Jones." When she told Mr. Fenton about the recipes, he said she must be keeper of the culinary keys of Tory.

"But Antha," Mother now protested, "nothing is going to happen to you and Will."

"You never can tell in these days of fast horses," Antha answered. "You know Will, and how he drives that team, especially when his dander's up."

"Mrs. Overstreet's got a great big new urn in her front yard and she's going to fill it with geraniums," I said, suddenly remembering I had news to carry.

54

"I knew she'd never rest after I got the new iron deer for my front yard," Antha snorted. "Just wait till I tell Will. He'll be sorry he opposed the deer when he sees what it drove Minnie to."

"She moved it in from their lot at the cemetery," I said.

"If that don't beat the band!" Antha threw back her head and laughed. "Robbing the dead just to show off."

"She's gilding it," I added.

"The fool!" Antha said.

"After she's through gilding the urn, she's going to go down and see the Baldwins. She asked Gracie if her mother and father were home. She's going to take them a green-apple pie."

"Green-apple pie! My foot! You'd think she invented it and was the first person to know the summer green apples were in. Why, I and Will have been eating green-apple pie for a week. She's got something up her sleeve or she wouldn't go traipsing up there with a pie."

"Maybe she just wants to give them a pie," Mama said.

"Kate Bradford, you know better than that." Antha turned to Mama. "She hasn't given you a pie, has she?"

"Of course not," Mama answered. She didn't mention that Minnie had sent us a jar of spiced pickled cherries the week before.

"Well, she'd better not, not when I live next door. I can make all the green-apple pies both our families need." Antha went out to look at the angel food. When she came back she had a plate of spice cookies in her hand. "Something to nibble on," she said, handing me the plate. "I tell you what we'll do. We'll carry the cookies in the parlor and raise the shades. When Minnie comes along with her pie for the preacher, it'll plague her to know why the shades are up."

"Oh goody!" I cried. "I love the parlor."

"Do you, dearie? I don't know why you and I and Will don't sit in there oftener." Antha led the way into this sacred room, carrying the cookies and a mug of milk for me, on a big black tin tray.

The gilded rolling pin fad was the last word in Tory. Almost all the women except Mama had one hung in their parlors. Gilded chopping bowls with nature scenes painted on them were also very popular. Mrs. Antha never liked to do anything in which she couldn't excel. She knew she couldn't paint *so* she went into Springfield and hired Miss Beulah Bickford to decorate her kitchen utensils. Miss Beulah Bickford was a true practicing artist. She gave lessons in china painting and charged fifty cents an hour. "Miss Beulah says I'm an art patron, whatever that is," Mrs. Antha had explained to me the day she drove home with her treasures.

Consequently, Mrs. Antha had what Mama called

56

a one-man show. There was a rolling pin with pink roses painted on the gilt, a chopping bowl ornamented with a weeping willow, a chopping knife with a waterfowl painted on its handle, a gilded egg beater with violets done on the pink ribbon by which it hung, a potato masher decorated tastefully with butterflies. But the greatest masterpiece from Miss Beulah's studio was the coal bucket which stood in one corner, as the room had no fireplace. This had a shiny black background and was executed, as Miss Beulah had said, in a snow scene. The snow glistened with mica, the sky was bright blue, and the man and the sleigh that were pictured in the center of one side dwarfed the house by which they stood.

On state occasions when Papa had been in the parlor, he would come away singing, "Things are rarely what they seem, skim milk masquerades as cream." And Mama was always quoting from her book with the pansies on the back, " 'Art is something you know to be useful or believe to be beautiful.' " Then she would add, "How that author would be confused over the useful rolling pin leading such a double life." But I loved the gilded rolling pins even if it was disloyal to the family.

This day I went on my usual round, looking at these painted objects, examining the hair wreath in its big frame and picking up the sea shell to listen to the roar of the ocean. Then I stationed myself at the window to watch for Mrs. Overstreet. In a few minutes, she appeared. "She's got something on a plate covered with a napkin. It's the pie," I announced.

"Don't fiddle with the curtains," Antha warned me. "We don't want her to know we're watching her."

We heard someone coming in the back door. "It's just Will," Mrs. Antha explained. He stood in the doorway. He was my year-round Santa Claus. Besides, he looked like that gentleman, for he had eyes that twinkled and dimples how merry, his cheeks were like roses, and his nose like a cherry.

"Why Miss Susan Dusanberry is here," he said pulling my braids. This was one of his names for me and it always made me giggle.

"Uncle Will," I said, "I've been waiting for you to come so I could ask you and Mrs. Antha to my party. It's all right if I ask them now isn't it, Mama? It's an unbirthday party but it's going to be as nice as a birthday party."

"Of course," Mama agreed.

"Mr. Fenton, you know — the funeral man — is coming down, and — "

"So I heard tell," Uncle Will said.

"And he is bringing me things for a party," I went on. "Enough for twelve. I'm going to have my favorite people. It's Friday night."

"That's mighty kind of you, but don't you want to have little folks?" Uncle Will asked.

58

"No, because Mama said there're so many more children than twelve in Tory. We wouldn't want to hurt anyone's feelings by leaving them out. You know how Gracie cried when she wasn't invited to Bessie Russell's party. I'm having Gracie, of course, because she's my best friend, but I'm having Mr. and Mrs. Baldwin, too."

"I'll bring an angel food with pink icing," Mrs. Antha said.

"I think Mr. Fenton is bringing little cakes," Mama said.

"Little cakes! They'll be just for show. You'll want something you can put your teeth into. You'd better get a rustle on and make a lemon jelly cake. And Will can make a big freezer of cream." Antha began making plans for the party.

"I can make the ice cream," Mama said.

"I never said you couldn't," Antha said. "But it don't just make good sense when we have all that cream from Captain January." Captain January was the Joneses' Jersey cow. They had let me pick out its name.

"Now, Helene, you tell Uncle Will about the goings-on up at Minnie Overstreet's," Antha said.

I repeated the story.

"She's going to just think she's in hog-heaven with that gilded urn! Now, we've got to find out what she's up to next, going up to the Baldwins with that pie," Antha added.

"Maybe she's ashamed because she took the urn off

Andy Overstreet's grave and she just wants to sweeten up the Reverend so he won't talk," Uncle Will suggested.

"Not on your tintype," Antha said. "Minnie Overstreet's not the kind to be ashamed. If she was, she wouldn't have pumped an innocent child and found out I was taking fifteen kinds of pickles to the fair last year and then took eighteen and got the prize."

"I didn't mean to tell about the pickles," I said.

"I know you didn't, dearie. Nobody's blaming you a mite," Mrs. Antha patted my hand.

FIVE

On thursday, three days later, mr. fenton
arrived. I had decided to give up trying to call him
Uncle Winton. He wasn't a cozy person like Uncle Will
and yet he was pleasant and didn't ignore me, as
some older people did, but not if I could help it.

Mama and I met him at the morning train. He was
loaded down with boxes, wrapped in shiny pink paper
and tied with ribbons.

"For your party," he said as he handed me one to
carry.

"Can I open them now?" I asked when we were home.

"They're yours," Mr. Fenton answered.

I was careful about untying the ribbons, for we
always saved ribbons.

"You did get the idea," I cried as I looked inside.
"My party is going to be just like the ones you read
about in stories!"

"How beautiful! Don't handle them," Mama said as
she looked over my shoulder.

"But the cakes and the bonbons would make such
beautiful ornaments to put in the parlor," I said as I

61

looked at the tinted frostings, pale pink, yellow, and lavender. There was also a box of paper hats, frilled nut cups, and a big package of Chinese paper lanterns.

"I'm afraid Helene thinks our parlor is too plain," Mama explained.

"I have something for you, too." Mr. Fenton opened his traveling bag and took out a package. It was a copy of Longfellow's *Outre-Mer*.

"Oh, a travel book!" Mama cried, looking at the index. "And such a sweet binding, white and green with gold lettering. It's sweet enough to be a parlor ornament. I like books for ornaments. It isn't just Helene who thinks my tastes are too plain. I'm considered queer in Tory because I don't have a colored glass basket and plates with red ribbons run through their edges. Not to mention gilded rolling pins."

"I know you read your books, too," Mr. Fenton said. "I almost brought you Richard Harding Davis's *Soldiers of Fortune*. Have you read it?"

"No, and I'd like to. Novels are so relaxing," Mama said.

"It's a good yarn. I'll send it down or bring it if I may?" Mr. Fenton said.

"Of course," Mama smiled.

"Frank will be home soon. He's excited about the fishing," Mama said. "I wonder if you really want to go fishing?"

62

"I wonder." He gave Mama an icing look. "But, of course I do."

"Frank is counting on it," Mama said. "He loves to fish but he rarely catches anything. He usually doesn't take anyone with him, even Helene. He says he goes to rest and commune with nature. He says that to tease me because I'm supposed to be the sentimental one of the family. I'm not really. But what am I saying? I shouldn't talk about myself and, besides, no matter how advanced women are becoming in this modern age, it isn't becoming for them to give up sentiment."

"You'd look pretty in anything you'd wear," Mr. Fenton said.

"Even bloomers?" Mama asked.

"Yes," Mr. Fenton laughed. "Anyway, I think sentiment is a word into which you can read your own meaning. I'm going to insist on thinking of you as sentimental."

"Mama's so pretty," I said.

Before anyone could answer, Papa came in the door. He was handsome, too. He was such a straight-up-and-down person.

"Did the Cooper baby die?" I asked.

"No, but it had convulsions. That's why I'm late," he said.

"Frank always has someone to worry about," Mama said. "I'll go and put your lunch in a basket."

63

"And I'll get some oats for the horse," Papa said.
"I watered him at the trough by the office. We'll drive
down to the river."

After they left, Mama and I went into the kitchen to
have some extra sandwiches she had prepared. "It's so
good for your father to have someone like Mr. Fenton
to talk to," she said. "He's a Republican and they both
take *Harper's Weekly*. Papa, too, gets lonely in his layer
of the lemon jelly cake."

"Is he in the same layer as we are?" I asked.

"Oh yes, we all are," Mama answered. "It's the Tory
layer."

"I like our layer," I said. "You and Papa, and the
party. I just have everything except a pony and a bicycle. After this, I'm going out and work on my clover
chain."

"Are you making it as a decoration for the party?"
Mama asked.

"No, it's a secret," I said.

"That's fine," Mama said and smiled. She never tried
to pry into my secrets. That's why I didn't ask more
questions about Mr. Fenton.

In the middle of the afternoon, Papa and Mr. Fenton came back. I ran into the house to see if they had
caught any fish. They hadn't. Papa rarely did.

"Any calls?" he asked.

"Yes, three, I have them written down," Mama answered. "But do stay and have some lemonade."

"Sounds good," Papa said. "Besides we haven't finished Teddy Roosevelt, yet. Winton and I are Republicans but we're not imperialists."

"We'll have our lemonade under the grape arbor," Mama said. Soon she came out with the pink company pitcher and its matching tumblers. Ice tinkled in the lemonade.

"The next door neighbors, the Joneses, gave us the ice this time," Papa said. "But you'll meet the Joneses at the party. I suppose you've explained to Winton about the party."

"I haven't had time." Mama turned to Mr. Fenton. "You wrote that you were bringing down twelve of everything. That certainly is a lot but there are so many children in Tory."

"That's Papa's fault," I said. "He just keeps bringing people new babies all the time."

"A bad habit of mine," Papa agreed.

"I tried a children's party once, for twelve," Mama said. "A whole row of children lined up on the bank across the street to watch. It nearly killed me."

"And then she ended up by asking them all over," Papa added.

"Well, I knew I could count on Antha Jones," Mama said. "I ran over to her house and, as usual, she had

65

cake and cookies. She came over and helped me and it all worked out. So Helene's asking older people."

"Anyway, I like all those big people I'm asking," I said. "They are all very special friends of mine, and I am having Gracie."

"She's Helene's best friend, the minister's child," Mama explained.

"You're not having Minnie Overstreet?" Papa asked.

"Oh, no." I was shocked. "Not with Mrs. Antha coming."

"Now look here, baby," Papa turned to me. "You mustn't take up the village hates. Mrs. Overstreet is one of my star patients."

"She isn't as good a patient as Mrs. Blankenbarger," I insisted.

"She doesn't have as many strange ailments, but she pays her bills promptly, in cash." Papa turned to Mr. Fenton. "Hate and jealousy seem to run high here. I think it's because we don't have enough interests. Minnie and Antha have been feuding for years, but they both like us. George Baldwin and I have talked it over. The minister and the doctor must always remain neutral. If I took sides, one of those women might die of apoplexy before they could send into Springfield for another doctor. Don't forget this, Helene. Kate's so tactful, she gets along with everybody."

"Minnie Overstreet announced last spring at the Ladies' Aid that children made her nervous," Mama said.

66

"I feel that's a good excuse for not asking her. I'll explain it the next time I see her. But she is good to Helene."

"That's because I'm Doc's little girl. Everybody looks up to Papa," I remarked. Somehow, I had a feeling that Papa should be built up. Mr. Fenton seemed to like him, too, but Mama was his favorite.

Papa smiled at me. "I must leave this pleasant company. Old Mike has had a rest now." Papa always thought more about resting his horse than he did about resting himself.

"We'll all carry our glasses into the kitchen," Mr. Fenton suggested. "Tell me more about the Antha Jones-Minnie Overstreet feud."

"It goes back to the Civil War." I knew he was talking to Mama but I didn't like to be left out.

"Yes," Mama agreed. "It started with their fathers. Antha's father got his start by driving cattle overland, selling them and putting the money in government land which sold for a song. Minnie's father came out, too, before the war. He saw what wonderful land it would be after it was cleared and drained. At the close of the war, they paid off some of the Northern soldiers with land grants. Mr. Watkins, that was Minnie's father, found out which company was getting the grants in this county. Then he bought up several trunks of new clothing for men. As the soldiers were being discharged, Mr. Watkins was there and offered to trade them a new outfit for their land grants. He was supposed to have stressed the fact that they wouldn't want to go home to their wives and sweethearts looking ragged and dirty, and that the land was far away in the prairies and filled with swamps and malaria. There was a lot of malaria out here then, the shakes, as they used to call it. You can see why many of the soldiers fell for Mr. Watkins's scheme. They were tired of being away from home. They didn't want to strike out into a new land."

"Mrs. Antha's father hated Mrs. Overstreet's father for this trick," I added.

"I should think so," Mr. Fenton agreed.

"The two families never got along," Mama said. "There was always rivalry. The latest is over the iron deer and the gilded urn."

"Tell me about that," Mr. Fenton said.

Mama told him about Mrs. Antha's deer and Minnie Overstreet's urn.

"Let's take a walk and view these beautiful objects," Mr. Fenton suggested to Mama.

"We might," Mama agreed. "But there's more to the story. After Minnie Overstreet had the gilded urn in place, she either felt a little sheepish about taking it from her husband's grave or else she wanted to put something over on Antha Jones, anyway she went down to the minister's and asked him to come over and dedicate the urn."

"And did he?" Mr. Fenton asked.

"Mr. Baldwin is very obliging and likes to do things the easy way. He didn't like to refuse but he did say he didn't think they should have a regular dedication service. He agreed though to come down by himself and say a prayer over the urn. He did it yesterday. I'll have to admit I got this part of the story from Helene. Gracie told her."

"And it's true," I said. "Gracie and I hid back of the snowball bush and saw him there with Minnie beside him. He bowed his head and everything. She wanted to have Mrs. Baldwin sing a hymn and ask people to come, but Mr. Baldwin said no."

"I'm going to take sides with the iron deer," Mr. Fenton said.

"Good!" I cried. "Now I'm going out in the meadow."

"We're having an early supper," Mama reminded me. The plan was that Mr. Fenton would go back into Springfield and stay all night at the hotel. He had some business to take care of at the State House, something to do with an insurance company. He would be back the next day in time for the party.

Mrs. Antha had sent over two fried chickens for our supper that night. She said it didn't make sense to come down into the country and not sink your teeth into some real good fried chicken. Papa always said if Tory ever adopted a coat of arms it should be emblazoned with a pair of crossed drumsticks. From late spring through the fall, fried chicken was served at all the church suppers, always taken to picnics, and appeared on everybody's Sunday dinner table.

As I went out to the little meadow, I took the clover chain from under the lilac bush where it was hidden. I picked a lapful of white clover, and sat down by a small tree to braid them. I was making a wreath to hang around the neck of Mrs. Antha's deer.

All this hootnanny, as Mrs. Antha called it, over Minnie Overstreet's urn had made me simply furious. It wasn't fair to Mrs. Antha's and Uncle Will's beautiful new deer.

Miss Rose, my Sunday School teacher, said that God listened to little children's prayers more than anyone else's. That gave me an idea. For a year I'd kept a prayer chart, punching it each night after I said my prayers. At the end of that time Mama had loaned the punch to a friend to use at a euchre party and never got it back, so I had lost interest in the chart. In fact, I'd been a little lazy about praying of late. But after all, Jesus still wanted me for a sunbeam, or else they were lying at the Christian church. I was a jewel in God's crown, to quote Miss Rose. He hadn't forgotten the prayer chart. He'd sent Mr. Fenton to us. Still, as I wasn't absolutely certain about my own pulling power, I had decided to make the clover chain to attract the Lord's attention.

Carefully carrying the chain, I went through the hole in the hedge, walked to the front of the Joneses' house

70

and draped the chain around the deer's neck. It looked beautiful.

There was nobody coming down the street, so I knelt in prayer, pointing my hands toward heaven. I was copying a picture hanging in our Sunday School room which showed a little blonde girl praying. I wasn't pretty like that child, but that was the Lord's fault. He could have made me look like Mama.

With all my planning I hadn't decided what to say. I couldn't race through the Lord's Prayer and add, "God bless everybody," as I had done when I kept the prayer chart. No one ever prayed out loud in our family and we didn't say grace at the table. But I had taken many meals with the Baldwins so I decided to model my dedication service on what Mr. Baldwin always said for grace. Looking around to see that no one was near, I intoned in a loud voice, "Dear Lord, we thank you for this bountiful deer. Make it sufficient unto our needs. This is the wish of your little friend, Helene Merriam Bradford."

I'll have to admit I felt pretty smug as I walked back into our yard. To my surprise Mama and Mr. Fenton were standing back of the hedge. They had seen me going over to the Joneses with the clover chain. Mama was wiping her eyes on a handkerchief of Mr. Fenton's. Mama rarely cried but lately she had been different.

"Did you hear my dedication service?" I asked.

Mama nodded. She put her arms around me and

71

turned to Mr. Fenton. "She's just a little girl. Sometimes I forget. And she does love the Joneses."

Later that day, I heard Mrs. Antha tell Mama, "I and Will heard Helene with the deer and we bawled like babies."

Everybody was doing queer things that summer.

SIX

Just as they were always saying in the Sunday School papers, the day of the party dawned bright and clear. At least every hour, I took out the guest list and studied it. I knew it by heart, but "consulting a guest list" was another phrase from the printed page. My list was written on a school pad and started: Papa, Mama, Mr. Fenton, Me. It went on to include Mrs. Antha and Uncle Will, the three Baldwins, Mrs. Huddleston and her brother, Wilbur, the inventor. He worked in a shed at his sister's house. He'd never been able to invent anything that had sold, but Gracie and I knew he would. We went to help him several times a week. He'd show us his drawings and let us polish pieces of metal with pumice stone. Mrs. Huddleston would bring out cookies for us. She loved Wilbur and didn't seem to mind having us around. We loved him, too.

I had wanted to invite Mr. Blankenbarger because he had bought Gracie and me the sodas in Springfield. Another nice thing about Mr. Blankenbarger was that we were always welcome to come into his hardware store and try on sunbonnets. Mr. Blankenbarger sold these because he carried work gloves for men and felt he shouldn't neglect the ladies. But Mama said you simply couldn't invite a man without his wife. Mrs. Blankenbarger was often sick but it wouldn't be safe to count on this when a party was in prospect. If she came, it would have made thirteen and no one in Tory would dream of coming to a party with that unlucky number. Besides, we had a dozen of everything.

My next suggestion was the barber, Ferdinand Fuchre, or Ferd as he was called, since few could master his last name which he said was Frenchy. He had other supposedly Frenchy touches, too, a black waxed mustache, pink cheeks, which it was whispered he touched up, and gay vests. He was always scented with violet perfume.

I was never allowed to step foot into Ferd's shop but I admired him from afar. He sang tenor in the church choir. Gracie's mother sang in the choir, too, and we often dropped in at choir practice. In this group Ferd was known as a card. He had a little feather duster with a gilt handle which he would whisk out of his pocket to tickle the women when they were practicing their solo parts. The old maids of the town, which meant girls around thirty, were all supposed to be in love with Ferd. They were always asking Gracie about him. But Mama said very definitely I could not have Ferd to the party because he wasn't like Papa and Mr. Fenton.

74

I had then decided on Canary for the twelfth guest. Canary Cummings was the one colored person in the village. She was the town's great curiosity since no other colored person had ever lived there. Besides, no one could ever find out anything about her life or why she happened to move to the village. When asked if she had ever been married, she always replied she didn't know. In a town where everyone knew what your grandmother had died from and how many quarts of tomatoes you put up each year, this was irritating. But everyone liked her.

Canary took care of our washing. When the other women found out the Lord didn't strike Mama dead for being so lazy, they began to hire her at house-cleaning time or when there was sickness in the family. Soon she was in demand for weddings, funerals, and church socials. Mrs. Antha hired her often. "I just wasn't feeling so work-brittle today so I got Canary to come and help me iron." Mama felt this was an excuse on Mrs. Antha's part to see that Canary made money. They worried about her finances — she never bought anything at the store except black-eyed peas and salt pork. When she was working out, she had good meals — always ate with the family. She was prouder than our family and the Baldwins and didn't like contributions. She refused to take home food.

Another peculiar thing about Canary was that she raised orris in her back yard. No one else had this species

75

of iris. She must have brought the start with her when she arrived in Tory ten years before. Some people remembered she came in a wagon which carried many sacks and bundles besides her few household belongings. She had divided and transplanted the orris until her back yard was now filled with even rows of the plants. Gracie and I always went down in the blooming season to smell the delicate white blossoms. Each year, she dug up some of the roots, dried them, and took them into Springfield and sold them to a drugstore. Both of our mothers kept powdered orris root in the house. Mama used it as a sachet, sprinkling it in the bureau drawers with her underwear and putting bags of it in the linen closet. Mrs. Baldwin combed it through her hair to take out the oil when she didn't want to give herself a shampoo. Gracie and I liked to think that the very orris root our mothers used had been raised in Canary's garden and pounded into powder at Dodd's drugstore, our chocolate-soda heaven.

It might have been because Mama had given Canary her start as a household helper that Canary was so fond of her and often referred to her as the Lord. I was cautioned never to repeat this sacrilegious title to the Baldwins for Canary came to church each Sunday, although she was not a member. She sat in the back pew alone. People often asked her to sit with them but she would shake her head in refusal. You always knew she was there as her voice rang out clear and true on the

76

hymns. She couldn't read but she had memorized the words of the songs.

Papa and Mama were glad I invited Canary. We all agreed that she wouldn't be allowed to wash dishes. Mr. Fenton, who seemed perpetually entertained by everything that went on in the village, seemed to think it a good idea, too.

That morning, there was a great bustle both at our house and the Joneses. Mrs. Antha had her two ranges going as she was baking both an angel food and a jam cake. This last was another of her specialties. It was made with sour cream and black raspberry jam and was as damp, heavy, and rich as the angel food was delicate, light, and airy. Today the angel food was colored pink and was to have pink frosting.

The Joneses had won the argument about who should make the ice cream. Uncle Will was turning the freezer himself. The Joneses kept a handy man, Spider Benson, and he usually did the freezing of what Mrs. Antha called "the cream." But on state occasions, Uncle Will turned the crank because Antha claimed that since Spider didn't have a lick of sense, he turned the freezer with jerks and the cream wasn't as smooth. Each time the freezer was opened, to see how the ice cream was doing, Uncle Will hoo-hooed for me to come over and taste it to see if it suited me. I had at least eight samples of the two gallons they were making. Mr. Fenton said it should be enough since that was almost a quart apiece.

Today, the ice cream tasted even better than usual. It was yellow with Captain January's thick Jersey cream. Uncle Will had made a trip into Springfield to buy the vanilla to flavor it as the Joneses' supply was getting low. They always bought this from a drugstore on the Square. It was extracted by the druggist from the vanilla bean. Mrs. Antha never approved of "store vanilla."

At home, Mama was making her famous lemon jelly cake. If life really were like a lemon jelly cake, as Mama had told Mr. Fenton, life was going to be as good as Papa had promised. He had said that the new century would be a time for us to enjoy the best of all possible worlds. Our wars were in the past and we had nothing to worry about. Today, the cake came out of the pans looking as light as ever and having its usual rich odor. Papa said Mama understood Mr. Ruskin and iambic pentameter but she also knew when the syrup for her icing had spun a proper thread.

The party was to be in the back yard. Most of this was in grass with a small plot at the end for flowers and the tomatoes. In the early spring, we grew lettuce, radishes and onions out there but Papa never bothered with the summer vegetables, for patients always brought us baskets of green beans, dozens of ears of corn, and great bunches of beets and carrots. This small plot was separated from the rest of the yard by a row of currant and gooseberry bushes. Near the house was a big apple tree. A long grape arbor covered the walk down to the garden

78

plot. Back of this was the barn and a lot for the horse.

Uncle Will and Spider brought over wooden horses and long boards and set up a table under the arbor. Mama covered the table with white crepe paper.

The food was to be kept in the house until it was time for the refreshments. Mama had cut new, long fringes of newspaper and tacked them up over the screen door to keep out the flies for she knew there would be frequent trips in and out.

We waited until Mr. Fenton came back on the afternoon train to hang up the paper lanterns since he had said he wanted to help.

Mama often said people didn't have enough fun doing the little things in life. We certainly had fun as we hunted for good places to hang the lanterns. Mr. Fenton seemed to make everything gay. Mama was excited ever since he had been there.

After the decorating was done, we had a pickup supper. There was cold fried chicken, left from the day before, canned salmon with parsley and lemon, a compote of pink, hard-boiled eggs which Mrs. Antha had colored by soaking them in pickled beet juice. These were always popular at Tory parties. Mrs. Huddleston had sent her brother down with two loaves of homemade bread and a jar of strawberry preserves. On the table was a covered glass dish filled with comb honey. Beside it were small individual honey dishes. For dessert, we had cherries which Mama had canned. At the last minute,

Mrs. Antha, who seemed to live in perpetual fear that we might starve, had brought over lemon cookies with scalloped edges.

I am sure Mr. Fenton enjoyed our home-cooked food. He always said so but he never indulged in such Tory-isms as, "I'm so full I can't move" or "My eyes were bigger than my stomach." Papa and Mama didn't either.

After supper, Mr. Fenton lighted the candles in the Chinese lanterns. "Each leaf is an emerald," Mama said as the lanterns swayed in the breeze.

"They've made the back yard into fairyland!" I cried. "All the fairies in *The Blue Fairy Book* are hiding, maybe, up in the apple tree."

"I never had a more appreciative audience," Mr. Fenton answered.

The party was to start at seven. Most parties did. Children were usually included and we were often home by nine or nine-thirty. Papa used to say that it didn't take them long to kill a cake in Tory.

The guests arrived, the men uncomfortable in their coats. It was very warm, but the polite thing was to wear them until the guests all arrived and then let the hostess tell the men they could take off their coats.

The women were dressed up in either their Sunday dresses or their best dresses. Everyone had a best dress which usually hung in a closet until it went out of style. Their Sunday dress was their second best. Mrs. Baldwin had on her light blue muslin and wore the beads which had been given to Gracie at Miss Lou's. Mrs. Antha had on a new dress that had just come from the fashionable dressmaker at Herndon's store in Springfield. It was made of lavender mull and had revers trimmed with lace insertions, a pointed vest, and a high lace collar.

"Antha!" Mama cried when she saw her. "You look beautiful!"

"Oh shucks, Kate," she answered, "nobody ever said I was pretty."

"And Uncle Will looks 'aristocratically athletic,'" I said, quoting a phrase I had read in a magazine story that afternoon.

"Why, Miss Susan Dusanberry," he answered. "What big words you've got!"

Mama wasn't as fixed up. She had on a white duck skirt and a white shirtwaist. She had told Mr. Fenton she wore this to show off the collar I had made for her birthday. Mama was always thoughtful. This collar really was a dreadful sight. I never could sew but Miss Rose, the Sunday School teacher, had helped me. We copied it from an illustration on the page called, *Useful Gifts,* which appeared in the Sunday School magazine. The collar was made of ribbon and lace whipped together and ornamented with pearl beads. As I was making it, I tried it on Papa, the cat, and Uncle Will.

Since it was my party, we were going to have games. Mr. Fenton had brought down a fascinating new one, pinning the tail on the donkey. For this Mrs. Baldwin got the prize. I wasn't sure she hadn't peeked from under the handkerchief which was tied over her eyes as she knew Mr. Fenton was furnishing the prizes. She squealed with delight when she saw hers and no wonder, since it was a beautiful little bottle of perfume with artificial lilies of the valley tied to it. Next we played hunt the thimble. Brother Wilbur found it on a nail in the grape arbor. The prize was a silver thimble in a tiny mother-of-pearl case shaped like an egg. When a man won this, it was considered the great joke of the evening. Next we played spin the plate and a question and answer game we had found in *The Youth's Companion.*

After this, the men gathered into a little group and discussed politics. Men and women did not mix at parties or church affairs in Tory. I could hear the men talking about Teddy Roosevelt, Papa's great hero. Both he and Mr. Fenton were mad because poor Teddy had been forced into the vice-presidency by a mean Mr. Platt. All the men at the party were Republicans except Mr. Baldwin, who always voted for Bryan because he was so religious.

The election was coming up that fall of 1900. Election years were fun. There was excitement at the school and Papa always drove Mama and me into Springfield for the Republican torchlight parades.

"Kate," Mrs. Antha said, "don't you think it's time we started to get ready to serve?"

"Canary, you stay out and play with Gracie and me," I suggested.

"No," Mrs. Antha said firmly, "Canary's a guest, just like the rest of us. She should help. But you little girls stay out from underfoot."

Gracie and I sat down in the grass and began practicing "I Don't Want to Play in Your Yard" and "Daisy Bell." We were often asked to sing so we wanted to be ready. But the song about Daisy and the bicycle built for two made us sad. We were both pining for bicycles.

Brother Wilbur came over and sat down beside us. "Since I'm an inventor, I don't care much for politics," he said. "But that Winton Fenton was saying two men got up a process once to extract gold from low-priced ore and it about changed the gold standard."

"Gee, that Mr. Fenton, he told me to call him Wint, always knows what's going on. He sure don't act like a city bigwig. Makes me wish I'd been a lawyer, myself."

"I'm glad you weren't," I said. We loved to go to his inventing shed.

"All that talk made me think what my panner's going to do when it gets going," Wilbur went on.

Wilbur's panner was to extract fool's gold out of coal. So far it was only a few drawings on brown wrapping paper. It would take two flatcars to move it when done. Even Gracie and I, who had all the faith in the world in Wilbur Newlin, knew it would never be finished.

By this time, we could see the three big cakes standing on the long table with the trays of little cakes and bonbons at each end. Papa and Uncle Will had brought the freezer of ice cream up from the cellar. Everything was almost ready. Then we heard the fire bell!

At one edge of the village was the little fire engine building with the big bell on top. It had a sign painted over the door, RESCUE FIRE DEPARTMENT, NUMBER ONE. There never had been a Number Two. In the building was one hand-drawn fire wagon.

Wilbur was a member of the fire company so he was the first person from the party to start running. The rest of us ran to the center of the town, Gracie and I in the lead. There we could see the smoke coming from the north.

As we passed the next block, I noticed men standing by a vacant lot. "It's only a grass fire," I panted.

"Oh, heck!" Gracie cried. "We never have a good fire."

By this time Papa, who could run fast, caught up with us. "They're beating it out," he said.

"We *never* have a good fire," Gracie repeated.

"Anyway, the fire engine has started," Papa said. "You girls will get to see that."

Everybody from the party had reached the fire. When the fire fighters pulled the engine to the spot, there wasn't a spark left.

As there was no real excitement, we went back to the party — that is, everybody except Papa and Brother

Wilbur. We all stood in the front yard talking to the people who came along from the fire. Finally Wilbur arrived, bringing news. It seemed when they were on their way to the fire, Sam, the oldest Johnson boy, who helped pull the fire truck, fell down. In the excitement, the rest of the men had pulled the fire wagon over him and had broken his arm. But it was such an honor to belong to the fire company that he had gotten up, run after them and caught hold of the rope with his one good arm. As soon as they had discovered there was no fire, Wilbur had hunted up Papa to take care of Sam. Papa had taken Sam to his office, which was in the center of the village, and was now setting the arm.

Poor Papa! This was the kind of life he always led. "By Jesus!" he often said, "just let me plan on something I really want to do and someone either falls down a well, has a bellyache, or has a baby."

"I guess we won't wait for Frank," Mama said. "I hate to start without him, but he'd want us to. Let's all go back to the grape arbor and have our refreshments."

And then the second great excitement of the evening started. Mrs. Antha was the first to reach the table. She screamed. We all hurried to where she was standing. The pink angel food was gone! The gold-banded chop plate on which it had stood was still there and none of the other cakes or candy had been touched. But the cake had vanished!

"It didn't walk off on two legs," Uncle Will said as he patted his wife's arm.

"Gosh blame!" Mr. Baldwin exclaimed.

"That Minnie Overstreet took it!" Mrs. Antha cried. "She's always been wanting my cake secrets. She's been dying to taste a piece of it for years and she's too proud to take a piece of it when I carry it to the church suppers."

"Oh, I don't think so," Mama said. "Antha, you never made a lovelier cake."

"Don't you think some boy came in here and took it?" Mr. Fenton said. "It was such a beautiful thing that probably he couldn't resist it."

"Why wouldn't they take some of those fancy candies, too?" Mrs. Antha replied. "No, it was Minnie Overstreet. She set that fire a-purpose, slipped down here and stole the cake. And I'm going to bring suit and hire you," Mrs. Antha turned to Mr. Fenton.

"Lawsuits can turn out to be pretty tricky things at times," Mr. Fenton said. "If you couldn't prove she took the cake, she might turn around and sue you for slander."

"That's right," Uncle Will said.

"I know you, Will Jones," Mrs. Antha said. "You're always trying to settle me down. I'm not going to be settled. I don't care if my preacher is here, I'm not going to forgive and forget. Of course," she hesitated, "I don't want to spoil Helene's party."

86

"Oh, I'm enjoying it," I answered.

"And so am I," I heard Mr. Fenton tell Mama.

"Well, if I can't go to law, let's all of us try to see if we can find out if Minnie stole the cake. Of course, I know she did. Now, Canary," Antha turned to her, "you're going down to Minnie's this week to iron curtains. Not that she couldn't iron her own curtains but she just has to do everything that I and Kate do. Canary, you look around very careful and see if you don't see a crumb of pink cake or icing any place."

"Yes, ma'am," Canary answered.

"You know you won't, and if you did you wouldn't tell," Mrs. Antha said.

"That's right," Canary said.

"If I had my big magnet and the cake was on a tin, I might slip down and try to draw it out of the window," Brother Wilbur suggested.

"You'd better keep out of this, Wilbur," his sister, Mrs. Huddleston, said.

"All right," Wilbur said.

"I don't suppose prayer would help," Mrs. Antha said, turning to Mr. Baldwin. "You did pray over her urn." She would always be bitter about that.

"I'm afraid not," Mr. Baldwin said.

"Mama says prayers never deliver the goods," Gracie said.

"I never said such a thing!" Mrs. Baldwin acted horrified.

87

"She did so," I whispered to Mr. Fenton. He grinned.

"You'd better keep out of this, George Baldwin," his wife went on. "Minnie Overstreet's a member of the church, *too.*"

"All right," Mr. Baldwin said.

The men's agreeing didn't surprise anyone, unless it was Mr. Fenton. I suppose in Chicago the men had more say-so, but in Tory the women ran everything.

Mama took the empty cake plate into the house, so Mrs. Antha wouldn't feel too sad, and came out with the big knife to cut the jam cake and the lemon jelly cake. She carried a basket which contained the paper hats and individual paper cups filled with salted almonds. The hats were in bright colors — red, blue, green, and orange — but the paper cups were as delicately tinted as the pink sweet peas and the pale blue and lavender morning glories which grew on a trellis by the back door. Mr. Fenton had brought all these treasures down from Chicago.

Mr. Fenton put on a red hat with white paper streamers down the back. He helped pass the favors and then sat down by Canary and visited with her, although I noticed that he kept looking at Mama.

We sat down in rows, admiring the flickering of the paper lanterns while we consumed great wedges of the cakes and many saucerfuls of ice cream. Everyone wanted to take the baskets, little cakes, and candies home as they were considered too pretty to eat. This embarrassed me for I felt it wasn't just the way they would do it in Newport and Saratoga Springs. But as it was *my* party I picked out what I considered was the prettiest of the bonbons, a pink one with a candied violet on top, and ate it. It tasted pink but I felt I had never been quite so fashionable.

About this time, Papa arrived. "Frank!" Mama cried, "I'm so glad you came before it was all over." She patted his arm.

"Broken bones, or dark of night, or sleet or snow, wasn't going to make me miss Helene's party," he said.

"Why that's part of what Mr. Fenton said about Harry Simpson at the funeral," I said.

"I'm not quoting it very well," Papa said.

"I wish Miss Susan Dusanberry would have a party every night," Uncle Will called as he was opening the freezer again to get some ice cream for Papa.

"I don't," Mama whispered to Papa. "Antha," she added, "tell Frank about the cake."

"Well, damn it to hell," Papa said when he heard the story.

"I guess Doc's about covered the subject," Uncle Will said as he handed Papa his serving. "Antha usually has the good ideas but I've got one now. Let's not anyone here give anybody else the satisfaction of telling about the cake being stolen."

Everyone seemed to think Uncle Will had hit on a splendid solution. If by any chance, Minnie Overstreet

89

hadn't taken the cake, she would have been delighted that a trick had been played on Mrs. Antha. If she had stolen it, she would have had a letdown feeling, if no one started to make trouble.

But somehow, this didn't satisfy me. After the guests had left, we sat under the grape arbor with Mr. Fenton.

"I wish Sherlock Holmes and Dr. Watson lived in Tory," I said. "They could dig up the corpse of the pink angel food cake. Maybe Gracie and I could work on the case."

"Now, honey," Papa shook his head. "You'd better do just as Uncle Will said and forget it."

"If you and Gracie ever get in jail, that is a case I might come down and try," Mr. Fenton said. "I guess I missed a chance to come back by not taking Mrs. Antha for a client."

"You don't need a crime like the theft of a pink angel food cake to bring you back," Papa said. "I — I just don't know how to say it, but we aren't exactly like everyone in Tory. Damn it, we need company from the outside world. Isn't that true, Kate?"

"Yes," Mama agreed. She smiled. It was one of those smiles that swept everybody into its warmth. But I noticed that her hand shook as she started to gather up the dishes.

90

SEVEN

Mr. FENTON STAYED ALL NIGHT WITH US SINCE there was no train back to Springfield after the party. It was very warm upstairs in the guest room under the eaves even though the windows were propped up with sticks. There was new white mosquito netting, but no breeze stirred it. Mama had put a palm leaf fan on the stand table by the bed, and Papa pumped a pitcher of water from the well and carried it upstairs.

I always thought this spare bedroom was beautiful. The furniture was painted, or grained as it was called, to resemble light wood. On each piece was painted a design showing blackberries with green leaves and tendrils. Mama had embroidered blackberries on the white lined splasher which hung back of the washstand. The wallpaper was yellow patterned with white daisies. There was plain cream-colored matting on the floor and fresh white ruffled curtains at the windows.

The two pictures Mrs. Antha had given Mama for the room, called "Wide Awake" and "Fast Asleep" were in the top bureau drawer along with a beaded comb case and another beaded article, a small case shaped like the

sole of a shoe in which the guest was supposed to put
his watch during the night. Mrs. Antha made frequent
attempts to pretty-up our house. Mama's excuse for not
displaying such presents was that they were too beautiful to use.

The next morning after breakfast was over and the
dishes done, I went into my room to make my bed.
Papa had started on his calls. Mama and Mr. Fenton
were in the sitting room talking about things I didn't
understand at all, things like mysticism and Mrs. Browning, and "Sonnets to the Portuguese." Then Mr. Fenton
had a great deal to say about the beauty of the natural
and a place he called Walden Pond. I didn't know of
any pond near Tory called that.

I was just tucking in the bedspread when I heard Mr.
Fenton lower his voice and say, "I have another confession to make to you."

I moved up closer to the crack in the door. Papa had
often told me that curiosity killed a cat, but a cat had
nine lives to lose, and I only had one, so I'd better be
careful. But I wasn't going to miss any conversation
which started with the word confession. This sounded
as if it were going to be something I *could* understand.

"What is it?" Mama asked.

"*I* took the pink angel food cake," Mr. Fenton said.

"You *did?*" Mama cried.

"I did it because of you." I could hear Mr. Fenton
moving his chair.

92

"I don't understand," Mama said.

"No, you wouldn't," Mr. Fenton said. "You're so sweet and kind — so selfless."

"No, I'm not," Mama protested.

"Yes, you are. Now look at me." I peeked through the crack and I could see Mr. Fenton sitting very close to Mama. He put his hand on her knee. "I know it was childish of me but when Mrs. Antha brought over that huge pink angel food cake and everybody made such a fuss over it, I was mad. There was your wonderful lemon jelly cake and no one said a word. I was jealous, for *your* lemon jelly cake!"

"This is so funny! It's terrible!" Mama said. "Everybody at the party knows how Mrs. Antha counts on praise for her cooking, why, she has to have it. And she's so good and kind."

"And you never demand anything," Mr. Fenton said.

"Oh yes, I do," Mama answered.

"What?" Mr. Fenton asked.

Mama paused for a minute, then she said, "I demand having my iced tea without sugar. That's very strange in Tory."

"A negative virtue," Mr. Fenton said. "Go on."

"I demand time to do the things I enjoy, like reading. I achieve this by not having so many things around the house to take care of, such as Mrs. Antha's gilded rolling pin. That's queer in Tory, too."

"But everyone likes you — loves you — and looks up

93

to you," Mr. Fenton protested. "Whether you think you're strange or not."

"Everyone likes Frank and looks up to him. I'm just married to the town, that's all. But I do love every one of those people who were here last night," Mama paused. "I'm still simply stunned about the cake."

"I'm ashamed," Mr. Fenton admitted.

"You should be," Mama said. "But — since we've been talking about the fascinating subject of *me*, here's a question that has always bothered me. I think I'll ask you."

"Go on," Mr. Fenton said. "I'm flattered."

"Do you think it's better to read books and magazines and find out what people in the outside world are doing and thinking, or do you think, if you can't live like the people you read about, it's better to be like Mrs. Antha and live in a little valley of contentment?"

"I think it's better to be exactly as you are. I wouldn't want you changed a bit, not a single curl on your head," Mr. Fenton said.

"I really meant this as a serious question," Mama said.

"I don't want to feel serious. I want to feel happy. I always do when I'm around you," Mr. Fenton answered.

"You should feel serious. You've committed a crime — the cake," Mama reminded him. "Now, what are we going to do about it?"

From my vantage point where I could both see and hear, I was beginning to wonder when they would get back to the subject of the cake.

"Oh yes, the cake," Mr. Fenton said. "I'm really ashamed."

"What did you do with it? And how did you get away with it?" For a while, Mama had been using her dreamy voice, now she was practical again.

"It was easy," Mr. Fenton said, "I slipped it into a box, one of the Chicago boxes. They were out there under the table. Then when you all started to the fire, I ran up to my room and hid it under the bed. I hope it's still there."

"I'm sure it is," Mama said. "Now let me think. Helene will be going out to play very soon. I suppose she's reading in her room. After she leaves, we'll lock the doors so no one can come in. Then you can get the cake and we'll burn it in the stove."

"Helene said something about burying the corpse," Mr. Fenton said. "But I believe burning it is better."

"I know it is. And we must be very careful not to leave a single crumb for Mrs. Antha is in and out of the kitchen all the time." I could hear Mama getting up, so I softly stepped over to the little rocker and picked up the copy of *Janice Meredith* which I had been reading.

"Helene." Mama stood in the doorway. "Why don't you go and get Gracie, and then perhaps go up and see

Wilbur Newlin. We never did thank him for helping us take down the big table last night."

"Shall I ask him who he thinks stole the cake?" This was supposed to be a leading question.

"I'd forget about that if I were you," Mama said. She wasn't going to tell me about Mr. Fenton stealing the cake! I looked at Mama; I had a different feeling from any I'd ever had in my life, a terrible feeling. Before this it had never occurred to me that we would have secrets in our family, unless they were about Christmas and birthdays. I ached inside. It was a new sensation. Before this I had never been snubbed or left out of things.

My feet dragged as I went out of the house. I wanted to sit down in the hammock and cry. But I couldn't do that. I must protect Mama and Mr. Fenton. It would never do for Gracie to come to our house and find the doors locked. I didn't know why but I was sure it would cause talk. And Mrs. Antha shouldn't come over, either. Gracie and Mrs. Antha were the two greatest droppers-in.

I ran next door, found Mrs. Antha and told her Gracie and I were coming over to see her in just a few minutes. Then I went in the other direction after Gracie. As I passed our house, I could see smoke coming out of the kitchen chimney, the cake was burning! In a few minutes the crime would be concealed and the doors unlocked.

96

I met Gracie on the street on her way to our house. "We're going over to Mrs. Antha's," I announced.

"What for?" Gracie asked.

"Oh just to talk to her about you and me doing some detective work on finding out who took the cake," I answered.

"Nobody's come around to confess?" Gracie asked.

"Oh, no," I said. I could feel my face getting red. I was a liar! But I was slightly comforted by the fact that none of our family believed in hell.

Gracie's situation was different. Her father believed that sinners burned through eternity. As much as I loved Gracie there were times when she did things that I didn't think were right. But she took the idea of the hottest of hells very coolly, although she cried like everything when she scalded her finger with boiling coffee. I took this question up with her at one time and she said, "Oh shoot! Mama says she and I will get into Heaven hanging onto Papa's coattails."

"Do you suppose Mrs. Antha has any of the ice cream left?" Gracie asked as we turned into the Joneses' yard. "Ferd came down to our house early to practice a duet with Mama. Papa had to go out in the country because Mrs. Anderson is very sick. Mama didn't have time to cook any breakfast for me, but I went out and had bread and butter and pickles and some cold coffee that was on the stove."

I knew Mrs. Baldwin hated to cook and that Gracie was always hungry so I answered, "I bet she has ice cream. Uncle Will took the freezer home. He wanted to leave it at our house but Papa and Mama wouldn't let him."

"Come in, girls," Mrs. Antha said as we stood at the door.

"Do you think we ought to do anything for revenge about the cake?" I asked. "That's what we wanted to talk to you about."

"It's awful nice of you little girls to want to take my part but I think Will's right. We'd better just drop the subject. I never gave up on anything before, but I guess just this once won't hurt me."

"Do you still think it was Minnie Overstreet that took it?" Gracie asked.

"In my heart of hearts, yes," Mrs. Antha said. "And do you know, I like thinking she took it. I wouldn't do such a thing. The beauty part of it is that I'm sure now that she'd stoop to anything to taste some of my angel cake and try to see if she can figure out why it's different."

This gave me a nice comfortable feeling. I loved Mrs. Antha. If I should tell her Mr. Fenton had taken the cake, she'd be let down. I certainly didn't want to spoil Mrs. Antha's pleasure.

Just then Uncle Will came in. "Why it's Miss Susan Dusanberry," he said, "and Gracie."

"Why don't you call me Miss Something?" Gracie asked.

"Well I will, honey, let me think. I guess I'll call you Miss Gracie Racie because you and Helene are always racing around town on your two feet."

"That's because we don't have bicycles," Gracie sighed.

Bicycles! How we longed for them! And yet somehow I didn't feel that we should tell the Joneses. They were too good about getting me everything I wanted. And they often bought Gracie presents, too.

"We just came over to talk about the party," I said.

"That was certainly good ice cream you made," Gracie said. I could see her looking on the porch where the freezer stood, covered with a piece of old red carpet.

"Well, thank you," said Uncle Will. "How about having a mite of it, right now? I'm hungry for ice cream, myself."

"And so am I," Mrs. Antha agreed. "Will, you dish out some for all of us. I'll get the cookies. Did you like those I sent over for your supper, Helene?"

"I just loved them. They've got scallops on the edges and they're filled with grated lemon peel," I explained to Gracie.

"Mama says she wouldn't grate lemon peel for Jesus H. Christ."

"Why, Gracie!" I cried. I could see Mrs. Antha was shocked, too.

99

"I expect your Mama was only joking," Uncle Will said as he carried the saucers out on the back stoop. He came back with them filled with little mountains of ice cream. We all sat at the kitchen table.

"Gracie, now you eat a lot," Mrs. Antha said. "You've got legs like toothpicks. And look at you, Helene, your eyes look like burnt holes in a blanket. I expect you had too much excitement last night. You'd better eat a lot, too. Will, you watch the girls' dishes and keep 'em filled."

"Isn't it nice that we have such good little friends as Miss Dusanberry and Miss Gracie Racie?" Uncle Will said after he came back from giving us a second round of ice cream.

Somehow, this made me want to cry. "You'd always love me no matter what happened?" I asked. I was still worried about Mama and Mr. Fenton having secrets.

"Of course, honey, what's got into you?" Uncle Will asked.

"Just as I said," Mrs. Antha moved the cookie plate nearer, "burnt holes in a blanket."

I looked outside. The sun was shining. A beautiful curtain of morning glories hung over the porch. Inside, Mrs. Antha and Uncle Will were smiling at us. The cookies were rich and crumbly. The new century was starting us on the best of all possible worlds. If Mama didn't want to tell me about Mr. Fenton taking the cake, I decided, it was just because she felt it was one of those grown-up things that children couldn't understand. I was happy again.

"Gracie, let's sing something," I suggested. "Let's sing 'Ta-ra-ra boom-de-ay.'"

"Go on," Uncle Will said. "I love to hear you girls sing."

"Now I'll tell you a funny riddle," Gracie said. She had been brought up to put her best foot forward. She wasn't going to let me furnish all the entertainment ideas.

"Let's hear it," Uncle Will said.

"Why do old maids always go to church?" Gracie asked.

"To see the fellows," Uncle Will suggested.

"You're warm, but that's not it," Gracie said. "They go because they want to be there when the hymns are given out."

"Well, that's good." Uncle Will chuckled.

"I think we'd better be going," I suggested.

"If you must go, take some cookies to nibble on," Mrs. Antha said.

"Thank you," we both chorused.

Then we each took one for the road and ran out of the kitchen. We sniffed the tuberoses in the south bed, admired the iron deer gleaming in the sun, and started down Main Street, the center of our best of all possible worlds.

EIGHT

In January magazines, the new year was always pictured as a lusty baby in a high silk hat. By the time the December issues finally arrived, the baby had turned into a feeble old man with a white beard, carrying a cane. This year, the baby was particularly important; not only was he the New Year but the New Century. There had been much discussion in the paper whether 1900 was the end of the old century or the beginning of the new. Our family took sides with the group who insisted that it was the beginning of the new one. I was glad we did. Perhaps that was why the summer of 1900 had been so full of adventures for the Bradfords. The baby year was now a half-grown boy and from the way things were happening he was a cross between Puck and Huckleberry Finn. With such characteristics, it did not seem strange that young Mr. 1900 called upon me to save Mrs. Blankenbarger's life.

Gracie and I called her Mrs. Hardware-store Blankenbarger. Other people spoke of her thus as there were other Blankenbargers living in the country near Tory.

Gracie didn't seem to like her but I did. She was a star patient and paid her bills promptly. Papa didn't mind taking her money; he said it wasn't any strain on her tooled-leather purse. Mama counted on her sick spells to put me through college and Papa promised he would never let her die. He didn't want to hear the whistling solos she had already arranged to have at her funeral.

On the fateful July day on which I saved Mrs. Blankenbarger's life, I was alone in the house. Papa and Mama weren't even in Tory.

The telephone rang. Just answering it was an adventure since we hadn't had ours very long. There weren't many telephones in Tory. I ran to answer it, grabbing the little box I always stood on so I could reach the mouthpiece.

"Hello." The voice was low and sad. It was Mrs. Blankenbarger. I could tell she was a very sick Mrs. Blankenbarger. "Is the doctor at home?"

"No, he's gone to the Horse-Thief picnic," I answered. She should have known the picnic always came on the third Thursday in July.

The term Horse Thief referred to the Antihorse-Thief Association but nobody in the village except Mama called it that. Just that morning she had corrected Papa on that point.

"By Jesus!" he had said rather sharply. "Why bother about the name? Nobody steals horses any more. They've all forgotten whether they're for or against the practice. Anyway, what difference does it make what you call a picnic as long as there's plenty of fried chicken? We never seem to have time for fun any more, unless it's when Wint Fenton comes down."

"I've made a lemon jelly cake." Mama tried to change the subject.

"That's just fine, Mrs. Antihorse-Thief. Now, does that satisfy you? Don't forget I'm secretary of this august organization."

Mama had laughed and nobody was cross any more.

"Is your Mama there?" Mrs. Blankenbarger asked after I'd told her Papa wasn't at home.

"No, she's gone to the Horse-Thief picnic, too," I answered. "This is the doctor's little girl. It's Helene."

"Yes, I recognized your voice." Mrs. Blankenbarger was almost whispering now. "Do you know if the new doctor who's settled in the Chicken Bristle neighborhood is at home?"

This new doctor was a young man who had recently moved to Chicken Bristle Junction, ten miles from Tory. Papa had always been the doctor for that section. He said he didn't want any young doctor messing around with his patients, for he understood them all. Mama and I couldn't stand the idea of another doctor taking away part of Papa's business. If he should become Mrs. Blankenbarger's doctor, it would be simply awful.

"No, he and his wife went to the Horse-Thief picnic with Papa and Mama. Mama said it's better to take them

104

along so if anybody got sick, they couldn't call the new doctor and let him get started with the patients."

"Your mama's a smart woman," Mrs. Blankenbarger replied.

"I'll say she is," I said. "She took all those courses from Chautauqua, New York, by correspondence."

"So I heard tell. Does she read out of books?"

"All the time," I assured her.

"You don't tell. I always wondered — " Here Mrs. Blankenbarger must have remembered the reason for her call, for her voice sank again. "I'm a very sick woman."

"What seems to be the matter?" This was what Papa always said before he began asking embarrassing questions about bowels.

"It's just as your Papa said. I told him I had palsy of the stomach and he said the shaking would make the milk I drank churn a ball of butter in my stomach. It's done it. I can feel the lump just as plain. I'm afraid I'll have to be cut."

"Don't do a thing until I get there," I said.

"What can I do?" Mrs. Blankenbarger groaned. "My husband's gone to the Horse-Thief picnic, too. I'm here all alone, a woman with a real bad palsied stomach."

"I'll be right there," I assured her again.

Wasn't it lucky, I thought, that I knew about Mrs. Blankenbarger's stomach? The day Mr. Fenton left after his visit when he brought me the party, I'd been in the

105

buggy with my father when he made his round of calls. When we passed Mrs. Blankenbarger's house, she called to us to stop and came out to the road to talk.

"Doc, I've got palsy of the stomach," she announced.

"That's strange," Father answered. "Let's see, doesn't Mrs. White next door have palsy?"

"Yes, but hers is only in her head, though she sure makes plenty of fuss about it. I guess you know all about it. She's doctoring with you."

"Yes."

"Hers shows," Mrs. Blankenbarger went on, "and she gets all the sympathy. But I always say your organs are more delicate than your head. I'm coming down to your office some day real soon and get some medicine."

"That's a good idea," my father then agreed. "In the meantime, I wouldn't drink much of that rich Jersey milk your old cow, Queenie, gives, or eat cream. If your stomach's so shaky, it might churn in your stomach and make a ball of butter."

"I won't, Doc," Mrs. Blankenbarger promised. "How'd you like to take home a jar of cream to your wife, since I'm not to eat it any more? Helene can come in with me while I get it."

I went into the milk house with Mrs. Blankenbarger while she skimmed off the thick, yellow, leathery cream and put it in a shining glass jar. The milk crocks stood in bright tin pans of cold water. There was a damp

106

stone floor in the little building. Everything about the place was cool and clean. I hated to go back into the brightness with the summer dust floating in the sun's rays.

"That Mrs. Blankenbarger!" Papa slapped the reins over the horse's back and we started. "I hope I've scared the living daylights out of her. She's always eating too much rich food. We'll enjoy the cream because we don't live on stuff like that."

We drove along in silence for a while. "Do you know Tory's really a wonderful place for strange ailments," Papa finally said.

"Is it?" I was impressed at that, and a little proud.

"It surely is. You know old Tom Doane who watches the crossing?"

"He's a good friend of mine."

"Well, he told me just yesterday that he was suffering from air on the lungs because he'd had to stand outdoors in all kinds of weather. And now Mrs. Blankenbarger has palsy of the stomach. I'm going to be a nationally-known doctor someday, I take care of so many strange diseases."

"You're the best doctor in all the world, now," I said emphatically.

"That's just what Doc's little girl thinks." He grinned as he reached over and patted my knee. "Helene, I can always count on you, can't I? No matter what happens?"

"Why, of course," I answered.

I remembered all this as I stood at the phone. I hadn't understood what Papa had meant at the time, but it must have been that he wanted to count on me when a crisis like this arose. How lucky it was I had been with Papa last week and heard about the case! It was what Mr. Baldwin would call "the hand of the Lord" working for me. And what was the best of all, I had thought up a way to cure her. Just as Papa had predicted, she had a ball of butter in her stomach. Poor Mrs. Blankenbarger! Hot coffee would melt butter. I knew this because Papa and I dunked our toast in coffee every morning when we didn't have company. The hunks of butter floated off in flat yellow patches. Mama despised this practice, but Papa said, home was where you could do as you pleased, and if it wasn't, that damn-fool motto, *Home Sweet Home*, had better be taken off the wall. This motto was Mrs. Antha's latest present. Mama had hung it in the kitchen explaining to Mrs. Antha that the kitchen was the heart of the home.

I was positive Mrs. Blankenbarger had coffee in the house but just to be sure, I ran into the kitchen and gathered up our can and the white granite coffeepot. I would have liked to take the black bag my father always carried on calls but it was the most forbidden thing in the house. I never was allowed even to touch it.

It was about a quarter of a mile to Mrs. Blankenbarger's. I ran all the way. Panting, I went into the

108

kitchen. It was a hot day but a low fire was going in the range. Good housekeepers in Tory always had a fire going. I poked it up, filled the pot with water from the sink pump, dumped in a lot of the ground coffee. Then I went to hunt Mrs. Blankenbarger. I could hear her moaning.

She was in the downstairs bedroom. Everything was snowy white around the bed except the blue wedding ring quilt that covered her massive frame.

"Oh, here you are," she groaned. "I'm a very sick woman, a very sick woman. Here all alone in the house, except you, child."

"Don't worry, I'm going to save you." I was a little afraid to touch her but I reached for her hand. Papa always patted me when I didn't feel well.

Suddenly, she looked very sick. She gave a great groan, "My heart! I'm dying!"

"Oh, don't!" I cried. I dashed to the kitchen. The coffee was boiling. I found a thick china cup, poured it full, added a little cold water so it wasn't too scalding to drink and ran back in the bedroom.

Somehow, I managed to prop up Mrs. Blankenbarger and began pouring the coffee down her throat. She came to with a gasp.

"It won't burn you. It's just to melt the ball of butter in your stomach," I assured her.

After a while, she did seem much better and said, "Child, you saved my life."

109

"That's all right." I felt pretty modest about my accomplishment.

Finally, she pulled herself up in the bed. "Say, child, why aren't you at the Horse-Thief picnic?"

"Personal reasons," I answered.

"Are you getting punished for something?" Mrs. Blankenbarger persisted.

"No, it isn't that," I said. "I guess you really know why."

"What do you mean?"

"I really stayed home because of Gracie."

"Why would I know about that?" Mrs. Blankenbarger asked.

"When you were too sick to go to the picnic because of your palsied stomach, Mr. Blankenbarger offered to take Gracie's mother. You know they both sing soprano."

"Sam Blankenbarger is a tenor," Mrs. Blankenbarger corrected.

"I knew it was something high."

"Go on," Mrs. Blankenbarger ordered.

It was easy to explain. Mrs. Blankenbarger knew as well as I did all about the Baldwins and the choir. But I did have a scoop of sorts. She didn't know that the presiding elder had sent word he was coming to Tory that day. As a consequence, Mr. Baldwin had to stay home and Mrs. Baldwin had gone to the picnic with Mr. Blankenbarger. I didn't understand why Gracie couldn't have gone with them. Three could always crowd in a buggy. I could see this puzzled Mrs. Blankenbarger, too.

For some reason, though, Gracie couldn't go. She had cried and begged me to stay with her and said if I would, her father'd give her the keys to the church so we could preach. This was one of our favorite games. We took turns being preacher and congregation.

"Preach?" Mrs. Blankenbarger interrupted, when I came to that part of the story.

Suddenly, I realized I probably shouldn't have told this to one of the church members. Just last week our whole Sunday School lesson had been about the church being God's house.

But I was in the thing now and Mrs. Blankenbarger kept asking me questions. I knew, too, it was a good idea to keep a patient entertained. I reached over and patted her hand. Then I went on to tell her about our favorite sermon, which was built around the text, "Ask and it shall be given you."

Gracie had chosen this because Mr. Blankenbarger had just given them keys to their closets. Before this, when the Baldwins had missionary societies and other church things at the parsonage, everybody went all over the house and looked in the closets. Papa said they were trying to sniff the air of sanctity.

"What does your papa mean?" Mrs. Blankenbarger said.

111

"I don't just know. I think it's one of his jokes."

"Does your papa think we church people are nosy? You mustn't forget we own the church parsonage," Mrs. Blankenbarger said. "But go on about the keys."

"I guess Mrs. Baldwin told Mr. Blankenbarger they looked in her closets. He said he'd give her the keys. He came out himself and fitted them."

"I wouldn't put it past him," Mrs. Blankenbarger said. "Go on."

"I've helped them throw shoes and clothes and things in the closets lots of times before people were coming. Now Mrs. Baldwin can lock the doors."

"What an example for you children! I always did know that Effie Baldwin couldn't housekeep worth a nickel."

"We all thought it was nice of Mr. Blankenbarger because he has the hardware store to fix up the keys. Papa said it was a labor in the vineyard."

"Another one of your papa's jokes," Mrs. Blankenbarger said. "He's a good doctor but it looks like he's got more jokes than pills. Does he tell this around town?"

"Oh, no," I assured her. "We never tell anybody about the Baldwins' keys or anything personal. I'm just telling you because they came from your store."

"I see," Mrs. Blankenbarger said firmly. "In fact, I see a lot of things. I'd better get busy."

She started to get up. What should I do? Papa always

said you should keep patients quiet. "You're not going to try to go to the picnic?" I asked.

"How could I get there? Sam Blankenbarger's got the horse and buggy." Mrs. Blankenbarger got out of bed. "I'm going to kill and fry a chicken for his supper when he gets home. That Effie Baldwin couldn't fry a decent chicken."

"Are you *sure* you feel well enough?" I was excited over my triumph as a doctor. I didn't want anything to happen to her.

"It was a severe spell of palsied stomach and I'd have died if it hadn't been for you. I guess you're about as good a doctor as your papa."

"Then if you don't need me any more, I guess I'll go over and see Gracie since I stayed home from the picnic to keep her company," I got up reluctantly.

"Yes, go and keep the poor child company. And I thank you for saving my life."

"That's all right," I said.

It was a noon picnic. Papa and Mama arrived home before supper. I simply couldn't wait to tell Papa about my accomplishment. I thought he'd be so pleased.

"Good God!" Papa sat down on the sofa and stared.

"You didn't? Oh, you didn't?" Mama kept saying, particularly when I came to the part about Mr. Blankenbarger and Mrs. Baldwin. She twisted her handkerchief. I recognized it as one Aunt Hattie had sent her

113

for Christmas from New York State. "Poor Effie! She's just a silly little thing," she added.

"And harmless," Papa commented. "I bet Sam Blankenbarger never so much as held her hand. He's probably just a little bored with a wife who's always sick."

When both Papa and Mama became so stirred up over Mr. Blankenbarger and Mrs. Baldwin, I remembered what Gracie had said about Mr. Blankenbarger being stuck on her mother. I certainly hadn't connected Mr. Blankenbarger's repairing Mrs. Baldwin's keys with romance. I had thought of it as a nice member-of-the-church thing to do and felt it would please Mrs. Blankenbarger to think she had such a kind husband.

Gracie had hinted to me, too, that Ferd, the barber, was stuck on her mother. But Gracie was always imagining things. Her make-believes were different from mine. She felt that her whole family had a corner on affection. She liked to make up stories about people being in love with them. Once she told me that Miss Rose, our Sunday School teacher, was in love with her father. I knew this was a lie. She had also said that Barbed-Wire Ernie, a little boy our age, was stuck on her, when the only attention he had ever paid Gracie was to kick her in the shins.

"You're right, Frank," Mama interrupted my thoughts. "Sam probably is bored. Helene, I've told you many times not to discuss people's personal affairs. Now,

114

about this palsy of the stomach?" She turned accusingly to my father. "There couldn't be such a thing."

"No," he admitted.

"Then she didn't churn a ball of butter in her stomach?"

I was terribly disappointed.

"I thought you and Mrs. Blankenbarger would both understand I was joking," Papa said. "She probably had an attack of acute indigestion. But don't you ever dare meddle with any patient again."

Tears started to roll down my face.

"Now, now, honey, don't cry. I guess the things you told her might have helped her. I don't believe she'll ever have a spell again on the day of the Horse-Thief picnic."

"Antihorse-Thief," Mama corrected him.

"You mean she won't be sick much again and I can't go to college?" I asked.

"Oh, I wouldn't worry about that," Papa said. "You just told us Mrs. Blankenbarger said I had more jokes than pills. Mrs. Blankenbarger's putting you through college was only a family joke. Anyway, she's always going to have a weak back, a bad side, shooting pains in her head, the grippe, or la grippe as she calls it, and lots of other diseases. She'll be hearing about floating kidneys pretty soon and that's going to fascinate her."

"Where do they float?" I asked.

"We won't go into that," Papa said. "That new doc-

115

tor over at Chicken Bristle is all the competition I care
to have without teaching you how to diagnose."

"Now don't ever tell anybody about how you tried
to be a doctor," Mama cautioned me.

"That's right," Papa agreed. "It just turned out
damned lucky this time. Wint Fenton says more things
happen down here in Tory than they do in Chicago.
I guess he's right." He turned to Mama and gave her
a long look.

"Helene and I both want you to succeed," Mama said.
"That's why she was trying to help."

"Nobody knows what success is," Papa said. "Especially when they're having it."

"Not even Mr. Fenton?" I asked.

NINE

THE DISAPPOINTING THING ABOUT SAVING MRS. Blankenbarger's life was that I couldn't boast about it. But, everything seemed to be turning out like a storybook in that exciting summer; the next day Mrs. Antha called me over and said she wanted to congratulate me for the feat. Mrs. Blankenbarger had called and told her all about it. I felt comfortably smug again.

"And the beauty part about it," Mrs. Antha said, "was that you didn't brag about it a mite. Why, I'd been scared skinny if Flossie Blankenbarger had of called on me to help her out when she was in such a fix. And here you came over last night to help Uncle Will and I eat up the food we brought home from the Horse-Thief picnic and you never said a word."

"I didn't want you to have me for a doctor instead of Papa," I said, and then somehow felt called upon to add, "That's a joke."

"So you don't want to grow up and be a lady doctor," Uncle Will said. He was sitting in the kitchen shelling corn for his chickens.

"Oh, no," I said. "I'm going to grow up and marry a

millionaire, live in Newport, and be just like Mrs. Astor."

"Now, Miss Susan Dusanberry, you won't get too hoity-toity for your Uncle Will, will you?" he asked.

"Oh, no," I answered. "I'll invite you and Mrs. Antha to come down for all the big balls I give."

"Umph," Mrs. Antha said. "I've noticed that those who think they've just set themselves down in a butter tub when they've married for money, don't always palm out so well."

I had a fleeting vision of Mrs. Astor sitting in a butter tub, wearing her diamond tiara. I knew that Mrs. Antha and Uncle Will weren't ever too enthusiastic about my dreams of having millions of dollars, but then neither one of them wanted a bicycle the way I did.

They didn't want anything they didn't have. When they had married, it had been the mating of a richly cultivated section of land with three-hundred and sixty black acres. Their fathers had been the young men who had gone West, young man. Uncle Will had no ambition to crash the new frontiers of big business in the East.

Women all over the country were reading with absorbing interest about the fancy dress balls of New York society. But not Mrs. Antha! She preferred to read in *The Tory Item*, a paper which appeared once a week, that "Mrs. Sam Blankenbarger spent the day with Mrs. Lillie Holser" or that "Mrs. Will Huddleston went into

118

Springfield on Wednesday to make purchases." Mrs. Antha's life was happily bounded by her two coal ranges on which she prepared food for her favorite form of society, the church social. These were her soirees.

"I guess you're right about money," I said reluctantly. I decided to change the subject. "Are you going to enter pickles at the fair again this year, Mrs. Antha?"

"I sure am," she answered. "That was another thing I called you for. I wanted to have you ask your mama if she'd come over this morning and help plan."

"I'll go over and get her right away," I said. "She's writing a letter to Mr. Fenton."

"He's a real nice friend for your papa and mama," Mrs. Antha said. "I always did say letter writing was like religion, most men took it out in their wives' names. Your papa lets her do the writing and thanking him for presents."

"Oh, he writes to Mama all the time," I said.

"He does?" Uncle Will asked.

"Well, why not?" Mrs. Antha frowned at her husband. "Kate Bradford's the smartest woman in this town, and Mr. Fenton's plenty smart."

"And she's the prettiest," Uncle Will said. "Present company excepted."

"What's got into you, Will Jones?" Mrs. Antha asked. "Now, Helene honey, you run over and ask your mama."

I went home and gave Mama the message. She was still writing her letter but she folded it up and put it in her little writing box. Uncle Will was right, she was the prettiest woman in the village, in the whole world, really. This morning she had on a light blue striped gingham dress which was the color of her eyes and of the forget-me-nots painted on the writing box. Her cheeks were as pink as the rosebuds which adorned the corners of the box.

We went in the kitchen door at the Joneses'. Mrs. Antha was sitting at the table there studying a cook book. Since I had been thinking of Mama's beauty, I now studied Mrs. Antha. Mother's eyes were bright blue and Mrs. Antha's black as the currants in her cookies. Mother's hair was more curly than usual because of the sultriness of the day, while Mrs. Antha's graying black hair was pulled up into an extra tight knot and bristled with bone hairpins. Mama's dress was a lovely color but Mrs. Antha's starched dark-blue calico looked nice under a red checked apron. Mama was never untidy but Mrs. Antha's greatest charm was her stiffly starched neatness. Dozens of times I had heard her described as neat as a pin. Why pins had a corner on neatness was something I didn't understand. No, Mrs. Antha wasn't pretty but neither was a cook stove and good things came out of it.

"If you girls are going to talk about pickles, guess I'll go uptown and play pinochle with Sam Blankenbarger," Uncle Will said. "Guess he's kinda in Dutch, driving out to the Horse-Thief picnic with the preacher's wife."

"Will Jones!" Mrs. Antha exclaimed. "What's got into you today? Must be the heat. You're getting as gossipy as old Tater Tayler."

"I didn't tell about saving Mrs. Blankenbarger's life," I hastened to assure Mama since the name Blankenbarger had been brought up.

"She sure didn't," Mrs. Antha backed me up. "It was Flossie Blankenbarger told me herself. She says Frank's pronounced she's got palsy of the stomach."

"Frank really didn't say that," Mama said.

"Oh well, she might as well think she's got that as anything," Mrs. Antha said. "I know you never talk about the patients and I admire you for it. But you know she's an awful old granny about her health. What I really wanted you to come over for was to help me plan pickles. I'm not going to let Minnie Overstreet beat me again at the state fair."

"It was all my fault last year," I said. "If only I hadn't told her you were going to take fifteen kinds and then she took eighteen."

"Never mind, honey," Mrs. Antha said. "It was just like her to pump a child. I'm not always asking the preacher to come down and pray over a gilded urn and feeling pious, but I wouldn't impose on a child."

"You're so good," Mama said. "I hope I never do anything you wouldn't do."

"Why Kate!" Mrs. Antha said. "You know everybody in town looks up to you."

121

"If they do, it's because I'm married to Frank," Mama answered.

"No, it's because you're smarter than we are, and we won't mince any bones about that. But I don't hold with telling people how much I like them." Mrs. Antha looked embarrassed. She opened the book on the table, and read, " 'Published by the Woman's Home Missionary Society of the First Methodist Church, Springfield, Illinois, 1900.' I just bought it from Miss Beulah," she added. "The women of that church all gave in their recipes, then they made them up in this book."

Mama took it in her hand and read aloud from the title page:

"There is a knack about good cooks
That never comes from reading books.

"See," she said, "that's what I've always told you. You know how to put in pinches of this and that. You have the knack."

"Shucks," Mrs. Antha said, "you've got all of us older cooks beat on your lemon jelly cake."

I hung over Mama's shoulder while she looked through the advertisements which were at the front and back of the book. One showed a picture of a woman wearing a skirt reaching to the floor, a fancy shirtwaist, and on top of this an apron. She was standing by a stove. "Just listen," Mama read aloud, again. " 'Over fifteen hundred Gas Stoves in use in the city.' Imagine!

122

Wouldn't it be wonderful to live in Springfield!"

"But you'd freeze to death in the winter without a range going," Mrs. Antha protested. "And think of the expense if you wanted to have one of those new-fangled contraptions going while you baked beans all day."

"But it says here," Mama continued to read, " 'all things considered, they are cheaper to operate than any other stove as the expense does not commence until you are ready to use it, and stops the *minute* you are through. No coal to bring in; no ashes to take out; no smoke, soot or coal dust to defile your house.' "

"I still don't want one. It's a silly book anyway. Some woman says to cut your cookies the size of a calling card. She's just trying to be highfalutin. And there's a doughnut recipe with only one egg in it. That woman's a fool, just a fool, even if she does live on South Sixth Street."

"Let's look at the pickle recipes," Mama turned the pages. "Here's something new, peach mangoes. You take out the pits, then put mustard and celery seed where the pit was, and stitch the halves together."

"Could you stitch them?" Mrs. Antha asked. "I never was any hand with the needle."

"Papa's got a needle for sewing up skin," I volunteered. "I bet he'd do it."

"I know he could," Mrs. Antha said. Then she lowered her voice. "I heard he performed that Napoleon operation the other day."

"Caesarean," Mama corrected her.

"I knew it was some hero," Mrs. Antha said.

"What was that?" I asked.

"Nothing," Mama answered in that tone which meant I was too young to understand. But I tucked the word away to look it up in the doctor book down at Gracie's. The worst thing about belonging to a doctor's family was that we didn't have a doctor book.

"What I think you should do is to make up some new pickles," Mama came back to this safe subject. "I was thinking the other day that you could cut some green pepper like ivy leaves and put it in with white chopped cabbage and call it Waverley pickles. Scott's Waverley Novels are full of ivy. Minnie Overstreet would never think up anything like that."

"I'll say she wouldn't," Mrs. Antha beamed. "Go on."

"I found a recipe called Longfellow pickles. I think that gave me the idea."

"Literary pickles!" I cried.

"Isn't your mama smart?" Mrs. Antha said. "Literary pickles will be just the ticket."

"I'll work on some more ideas," Mama said. "There's a part in Keats's 'The Eve of St. Agnes' where the lover brings 'candied apple, quince, and plum, and gourd.' "

"Do you suppose we could pickle gourds?" Mrs. Antha asked. "Will's got a lot of green ones out on the vine by the woodshed."

"I don't know but we could combine the apple, quince

124

and plum and make a sweet pickle and call it St. Agnes's Eve," Mama suggested. "And we'll think about the gourds."

"It was the best thing that ever happened to this town when you moved into it." Mrs. Antha reached over and patted Mama's shoulder. "Minnie just thought she was in hog heaven last year winning the prize. This year, we'll show her. I've got to beat her, especially since she stole my cake at Helene's party."

"We don't know she stole it," Mama said.

I looked at Mama. Surely she was going to tell Mrs. Antha, now that it was all over, that Mr. Fenton had taken the cake. But Mama didn't say a word.

Papa had once said that most people had feet of clay but that Mama didn't even have a little toe of clay. There must be some very good reason why she didn't want Mrs. Antha to find out. It was probably because Mr. Fenton was coming down to Tory again and she wanted him to have a good time. He wouldn't have nearly as good a time if our friends didn't like him.

"Umph," Mrs. Antha replied to Mama's answer.

"I also have another idea," Mama went on. "And that is to make a pickle relish called Patriotic Pickle. It could be made of chopped white cabbage put in the jar in layers. The first layer could be colored red with beet juice, then the plain white layer, but I don't just know how we'd get the blue layer."

"It would be beautiful," Mrs. Antha agreed, "but what about the blue layer?"

"I had thought of using bluing to color the cabbage for that layer but the judges do have the right to open any of the pickles and taste them."

"And they just might, with anything that pretty," Mrs. Antha said. "Do you suppose bluing is poison?"

"That's just what I wondered," Mama said. "I tell you what, Frank will know. Helene, you run up to the office right away and ask him."

"Yes, you scoot up," Mrs. Antha turned to me, "and when you get back, I'll give you some chocolate blanc-mange. I and Will just got hungry for chocolate blanc-mange."

"Is it in the fish mold?" I asked.

"Of course, honey. You don't think I and Will would eat it any other way except in that mold you like it in?"

"It's simply dreadful the way you spoil her," I heard Mama say as I left.

Mama always used the verb run. I was always told to run upstairs, run down to the office, run over to Mrs. Antha's, and I usually did run. Today I ran very fast for, although it was only a block, I knew it was important to get this information about the red, white and blue pickles so Mama and Mrs. Antha could go on planning more exciting entries for the prize at the fair.

The office was a small wooden building next to the

126

grocery store. A tin awning joined the two structures. Papa owned the office. It was one of his favorite jokes that he was a capitalist because he owned business property in Tory. When he became even richer, he said he was going to buy the store building since they were united in holy matrimony by a tin roof.

There were only two rooms in Papa's little building. I went panting into the front one, the waiting room. It was always hot in July but today was what was known as a scorcher. But the office always had a cool, mouth-washy smell. I took out a handkerchief from the pocket set in the seam of my skirt and mopped my face, glad to be out of the sun. The door into the back room was closed, so that meant a patient was there.

The front room was never neat for Papa wouldn't allow Mama or Canary to clean it. Occasionally he swept and dusted it himself, but he never cleaned up the table in the center of the room. It was littered with pamphlets, mostly about fruit farming which was Papa's dream occupation. When he retired he was going to be a fruit grower.

There were calendars on the wall for people to look at. Mama wouldn't hang them up but Papa did although he never tore off the months. It was always January in the office.

Besides these, there was a page from a Springfield newspaper pinned in a conspicuous place. This contained a large advertisement for patent medicine. At the top of it was a picture of a huge, healthy-looking woman. Underneath was a letter which read:

Dear Sirs,
  I had doctored with Dr. B– for years and he didn't help me. I had bad pains in my back and had to get up nights and I was a sufferer from bearing-down pains. I was helped by one bottle of your Indian Tonic and now I take it regularly and am cured.
  Signed and sworn to by Mrs. G– T–. (Name furnished on request.)

Papa was the Dr. B– of the letter and the woman who wrote it was Mrs. George Tribble, who lived near Tory in the Horse Creek neighborhood. The advertisement infuriated Mama and me but Papa thought it was funny. Mr. Fenton had thought it was terribly funny, too. Papa insisted on keeping it up for what he called a horrible example to any other patient. It worked. No one from Tory ever wrote to the paper again.

The consultation room was different; there were no unnecessary things around. I think Papa cleaned it up every day. It looked more like Papa for he was very neat in his own appearance. All year round he wore seersucker coats in the office. There were always snowy towels on the tables under the instruments and a row of them hanging on a rack. Canary did the office laundry, carrying home a great bundle every week. It was only the front room which was dusty and untidy.

As I waited, I picked up a pamphlet on the care of Silver Spangled Hamburgs, an esoteric breed of chickens Papa was going to raise under his Ben Davis apple trees.

Soon the door opened and Papa was bowing out Mrs. Weaver Jordan, who had broken her wrist chasing a cow. Knowing just what was the matter with everybody was part of the fun of being the doctor's daughter. Papa always escorted his patients to the door and if he felt sorry for them he patted them on the shoulder.

"What is it, Helene?" Papa saw me and stopped short. I was never sent to the office unless it was for something very important. Our only telephone was at the house but I didn't relay messages unless they were vital.

"Is bluing poison?" I asked in a whisper. I didn't want Mrs. Jordan to hear about Mama's and Mrs. Antha's scheme.

"What's happened?" he cried. "Who wants to know?"

"Mama," I answered in a low tone, pointing to Mrs. Jordan.

"Where is she? Good God, speak up!" Papa cried.

"At Mrs. Antha's," I said. By this time I was definitely trying to be dramatic.

"Good God!" he said again, pushing past Mrs. Jordan at the door. He started running down the street. I ran after him calling, "It's just pickles!" But he didn't turn around. Papa was thin and had long legs and I couldn't catch up with him.

As I passed Mr. Blankenbarger's store, Uncle Will

129

came dashing out. He had seen Papa running with me following. "What's happened?" he called to me.

"Poison! At your house!" I yelled, as I kept going.

Uncle Will started to run, too. Uncle Will was short and fat and he couldn't catch up with me. I heard him trip and stumble on the new board by the barber shop. New boards on the sidewalks were something to wish on, like haystacks and white horses. Gracie and I had wished on this one for bicycles every day since it had been put down a week before. We knew it was higher than the rest of the walk but poor Uncle Will didn't.

By the time Papa arrived at the Joneses' kitchen, I was right at his heels. "What's happened?" he cried.

"Why not a thing," Mama said. "What's happened to you?"

"Did you drink bluing?" Papa's voice was high with excitement and anger, too, as he looked at Mama sitting by the window, calmly drinking a glass of iced tea.

"Of course not, Frank. What did Helene tell you?"

"I didn't tell him a thing," I cried. "I just asked, was bluing poison?"

By this time Uncle Will was in the kitchen. Three little boys who had joined in the chase stood on the back porch.

Uncle Will surveyed the scene. Mrs. Antha was on her way to the ice chest with the pitcher to get more tea, Mama was sitting there quietly and Papa was still furious. "What's up?" he gasped.

130

"Sit down everybody," Mrs. Antha called. "We'll explain."

"Damn it to hell! No!" Papa cried.

"Frank," Mama said, "you're speaking to Antha."

"Did you drink bluing?" Papa asked, walking over to where Mama sat.

"Of course not," Mama said. "We merely wanted to color some white cabbage with bluing to make some red, white, and blue pickles for the state fair."

"So they could get the prize," I volunteered.

"Be quiet," Papa said, turning to me. He was rarely cross with me so I subsided.

"Come on now, Frank, and have some nice, cool tea," Mrs. Antha said. Her remedy for any crisis was to eat or drink. "I'll give those kids outside some cookies and tell them nothing happened. We didn't mean to scare you, Frank. We were just satisfying our curiosity about using bluing in pickles."

At that the telephone rang. Uncle Will answered. It was Mr. Blankenbarger calling from the store to find out what was the matter.

"Not a thing," I could hear Uncle Will say. "Kate's over here. I don't just know what's up but I guess they must have spilled some bluing and sent Helene up to ask if it was poison. Guess Frank heard the word poison and got scared. Everybody's sitting around fat and sassy, as far as I can make out."

Then I could hear Mr. Blankenbarger's voice but

131

couldn't make out the words. Sometimes I could hear both ends of a conversation.

"Yes, I expect everybody did get excited, seeing us all on the run," Uncle Will went on. "Just tell everybody it's nothing, nothing at all. I bet I tipped over the cards. I'll come up this afternoon and we can start a new game."

"Seems like everybody's deviling Sam to find out what happened," Uncle Will explained to us. "Mrs. Weaver Jordan came down from the office to find out, too."

"I'm sorry I went off half-cocked." Papa walked over and put his hand on Mama's shoulder. "I was frightened." He tilted up Mama's chin. I thought he was going to kiss her, but he didn't. "I love you," he said to her.

Mama looked embarrassed. They didn't carry on, as Gracie called it, in public. "You still haven't answered our question. Is bluing poison?"

"How would I know?" Papa said. "I never had any patients who were damn fools enough to even think of coloring cabbage with it."

"Doc, they're sure a team," Uncle Will said. "That Antha of mine and your Kate. I guess you know they're planning and plotting against beating the bustle off Minnie Overstreet at the fair."

"We've thought up simply wonderful kinds of pickles to make," Mama said.

132

"Sit down, Frank," Mrs. Antha said. "Nobody can think standing up. And have a nice glass of tea. I've got some blancmange on ice, too."

"Just tea, thank you." Papa pulled up a chair. He reached for the sugar bowl and put two large spoonfuls of sugar in his glass. Uncle Will added four spoonfuls to his and stirred it vigorously.

"See," Mama turned to Papa. "Will stirs up his sugar. He doesn't waste it in the bottom of his tumbler."

It wasn't like Mama to pick at Papa before company. In fact, she rarely criticized him. He never made any suggestions to her, at least before me.

"Mr. Fenton doesn't take any sugar in his coffee or tea. It's more continental and fashionable," I said.

"You don't tell," Mrs. Antha said.

Everybody laughed, but I could tell they weren't amused, particularly Mama and Papa. Mrs. Antha, who thought it was worse to be highfalutin than to say bad words, laughed because she didn't want me to be scolded and Uncle Will laughed because I was Miss Susan Dusanberry.

"I like that Wint Fenton," Uncle Will smiled at me. "I always do say he's just as common as an old shoe." It was his highest form of compliment so I felt I hadn't disgraced this charming and delightful man who seemed to be adding so much to our lives, particularly to Mama's.

She and Mr. Fenton wrote to each other all the time

now. He had been to see us three times — once for the
funeral, and once to go fishing and bring my party. The
third time he came out to spend the day after he'd finished some law business. He had a case which he said
would be bringing him to Springfield from then on.

"I like him," Papa said. "And he surely enjoys Tory."

"Who wouldn't?" Mrs. Antha said. "He would be
plumb crazy if he didn't like Tory. If he wants his tea
to taste bitter like medicine, that's his business."

"Remember that lecturer at the church?" Uncle
Will said. "He said Tory was the buckle on the cornbelt. I thought that was real cute. It's a pretty little
burg."

"Yes," Papa agreed. "But as much as we all like
Tory, I can't sit here and let the inhabitants die off
like flies, as good as this iced tea tastes on a blistering
morning. And now, as for you girls, if you're doubtful
about anything being poison, by Jesus, don't ever mix
it in with pickles, as much as you want to win that
three-dollar prize."

"Antha *has* to beat Minnie," Mama said.

"Minnie's a patient," I reminded her.

"Thank God, we're among friends," Papa said. "Patients aren't everything in our lives. I guess the only
cure for you, young lady, to keep you from being a
complete smart aleck is to grow up."

This definitely wasn't my morning. I'd scared Papa
to death saying poison, then I'd been tactless about

134

the sugar and now Papa was annoyed at me again.

"Wint Fenton's coming down to the fair," Papa said, as he stood in the doorway. "I know he'd like to see you win, Antha, no matter what crazy pickles you and Kate concoct."

I could see Mrs. Antha and Uncle Will exchanging glances. I hadn't known this fact either, but I was sure Mama had, just from the way she looked. But I wasn't going to worry because she hadn't told me. It would be such fun having Mr. Fenton with us at the fair! "Oh goody!" I cried. "I bet he'll buy me lots of rides on the merry-go-round."

But again I'd been tactless. Uncle Will always bought me all the rides I needed on the merry-go-round. I didn't want him to be jealous of Mr. Fenton. This had seemed such a glorious and unusual summer, and it was only halfway through. What would the rest of July and August bring? But as Miss Rose always said at Sunday School, you needed dark days to appreciate God's sunshine. This must be one of my dark days.

"You'd better stay and have some blancmange. I was going to get it out for a little treat," Mrs. Antha said to Papa as he got up to leave.

"I'm afraid I can't," Papa answered.

That was like poor Papa. He never could wait for the real goodies of life.

"Poor Frank," Mama said as she watched him go

around the house. "He didn't stop to put on his hat when he ran down here. I hope he doesn't get a sunstroke. I never saw the sun shine any brighter. If only we could have a thunderstorm to break this heat."

I wondered if she, too, felt she needed a dark day.

TEN

THE VERY NEXT DAY, SOMETHING ELSE EXCITING happened but this time it happened to Gracie. Mr. Blankenbarger gave her, just gave her without her paying a nickel for it, a brand new bicycle! He said he had ordered it for her because she was his pastor's daughter.

When I was getting the mail, I heard some men at the post office talking about it.

"Why did Mr. Blankenbarger *really* give Gracie the bicycle? Why — " I asked Mama when I came home. The men at the post office didn't understand and neither did I.

"Because she's his pastor's daughter, just as he said," Mama answered.

That afternoon, Mama and I were pulling dandelions in our front yard when Minnie Overstreet stopped by. She started right in with the question, "Do you think Sam Blankenbarger gave Gracie that brand new bicycle just because he belongs to their church? That's what he's claiming."

"It's nice for Gracie." Mama motioned for me to

137

go into the house but I pretended not to notice.

"I think he's doing it to spite Flossie Blankenbarger. She's telling everybody how she nearly died when he was off to the Horse-Thief picnic with Effie Baldwin."

"But Mrs. Blankenbarger was sick that day and couldn't go," Mama said. "That's why he didn't take her."

"Most men stay home with their wives when they're sick," Minnie Overstreet said. "You know that. You'd have thought he'd have given Helene one for saving Flossie's life."

Mama reached down and pulled a clump of crab grass.

"I see you're not going to take sides," Minnie went on. "As for me, I think Sam's stuck on that Effie Baldwin and just trying to cozy up to the family."

"Helene, you run in the house and get me a handkerchief," Mama said.

By the time I got back, she and Mrs. Overstreet were talking about the weather.

"Do you think Mr. Blankenbarger is stuck on Mrs. Baldwin?" I asked Papa that night when he came home for supper. If Mama didn't want to talk about why Gracie got the bicycle, maybe Papa would.

"I don't know," Papa said. "You know that term, 'stuck on,' originated at candy pulls. A boy would get stuck on a girl because they were pulling candy together and the taffy stuck him to her. But I don't think

138

Sam Blankenbarger has been pulling any candy with Effie Baldwin lately. No, I'd say he wasn't stuck on her."

"I don't see why people can't realize that Mr. Blankenbarger is a nice, kind-hearted man and fond of children and let it go at that." Mama had come into the room.

"He was good to us when he bought the chocolate sodas the day we went to the hoarfrost house," I said. "You ought to let me tell people about that."

"No." Papa sat down in his chair and picked up the paper.

Gracie spent all her time on her bicycle. I'd never have her for a friend again if I didn't get one, too. Tears came into my eyes every time I thought about it. I must have a bicycle! Gracie was always quoting her mother in saying that prayers didn't deliver the goods, so there was no sense in getting down on my knees. There was no chance of Papa's going into the ministry and having someone give one to me because I was a preacher's daughter; I'd have to earn the bicycle myself.

I thought up several schemes to make money. One was to urge Brother Wilbur to invent something and make me a partner. It must be something big like a telephone that connected with the stars. Everybody was wondering about the stars and who lived on them. But where would we string up the wires? Even Brother Wilbur might not think it was practical.

I'd better think up something more like Tory. I wasn't allowed to bother people by selling bluing from door to door or taking magazine subscriptions but I decided it would be all right if I made something to sell in stores. I thought of the hatpin holders. I had made one as a Christmas present for Miss Rose, my Sunday School teacher, and it had been a great success. Herndon's store in Springfield would probably love to handle such pretty things. They were made of bottles, covered with organdy and lace. The hatpins were put in the bottles and hung up by a ribbon. Papa had lots of old medicine bottles and Mama had a scrap bag so my materials would cost nothing. I got out an old shoe box to hold my supplies and a notebook given to Papa by a hiccup remedy company in which I was going to write down my profits.

Although I still ached for a bicycle, after I started working on my first hatpin holder I felt better. Maybe I was getting like Mrs. Antha. She said work was good for what ailed you, and that you never got over trouble until you got to feeling work-brittle again.

Mama and Papa were both work-brittle people, at least they were always busy. I would be like them. I'd work my fingers to the bone like martyrs did. Sunday School had taught me how beautiful it was to be a martyr.

140

I was slow and awkward about sewing. It was two days before I finished my first holder. I wasn't too proud of it. The next one I made wouldn't be soiled and crumpled. When I showed it to Mama she said she would see about having it sold at Herndon's. A *would see* usually meant Mama wasn't going to do it. But since I was in a will-to-triumph mood I wasn't downcast. It was too late in the day to start another holder, so I went in and played with our Whitley Exerciser. The Whitley was something Gracie *didn't* have and something I had never enjoyed before.

The exerciser was a present to Mama from her father. Mostly it was elastic cords which ran over pulleys and had handles at the ends. Its frame was screwed on one of the closet doors. The directions, tacked up beside it, said it would expand the chest and bring physical perfection. The price was printed on the sheet. Five dollars! How that would have helped my bicycle fund!

Mama didn't care for the exerciser, either, and rarely used it. But Grandfather was like that. He was fascinated with new things. He lived alone in his big house in Michigan with just a housekeeper to take care of him since Grandmother had died. He was retired and he had time to read and study, and take up any fad which struck his fancy. Building a good physique was one of his latest hobbies. Besides the exerciser he had sent Mama a magnetic pad to place between the shoulders to give a good posture. This was because he was interested in a new ism — galvanism. She never wore the pad. His latest present had been a pair of health shoes which laced almost to the knees. Mama never wore these, either.

I just knew Grandfather would send me a bicycle if I'd write and ask him for one. Then there were Mrs. Antha and Uncle Will and Mr. Fenton. Gracie always said he was terribly rich. But I was never allowed to ask for things, even an important thing like a bicycle. Mr. Fenton was always sending presents. He was the best bet.

It was late afternoon and still hot. Perspiration ran down my face as I pulled and stretched at the Whitley exerciser. Mama was sitting on the front steps, fanning. Suddenly she called, "Oh, Helene, come quick!" I ran to the door. Papa was coming down the street wheeling a bicycle! It was a girl's bicycle, just like Gracie's, only this one was red where Gracie's was blue. My heart stood still. It couldn't be mine. Papa must have found it on the street and was bringing it home for safekeeping until the owner showed up.

"Is there a little girl who lives here by the name of Helene Bradford?" he called to us.

"Yes," I said in a little voice.

"I have a present for her," he said.

I jumped off the steps. Mama got up. We ran to the gate.

142

"It's from Mr. Fenton!" I cried.

Papa just stood there. A butterfly flitted onto the handle bar.

Mama burst into tears. "Oh, no, Frank, no!" she sobbed.

"Kate! She's only a child. How would she know?"

"I don't care! He can *never* come here again!"

"Helene didn't know," Papa repeated. "After all, Wint's a friend of the whole family. Isn't he?"

"Yes." Mama wiped her eyes. "But how could we have let her think that Wint was — that everything — that — " Mama usually was so sure of herself. "No, Frank, he can't come again. Or write."

I didn't understand. "We won't have to burn up the bicycle like the beads from the hoarfrost house, will we?"

"No," Mama said. "The bicycle's from Papa."

"Oh, Papa!" How terrible I'd been not to realize it! How awful to think my own Papa couldn't buy a bicycle, but Mr. Fenton could.

Papa leaned the bicycle on the fence. I put my arms around him and kissed him.

"You and your mother don't have to prove you love me. I already know that . . . I think." Papa's voice sounded as if he were talking to someone who wasn't even there.

"It's beautiful." I felt the handle bars. "It feels good." Then I turned to Mama. "I'm going to use my hatpin

143

money to buy a bicycle for you. Now that you won't be spending your time writing to Mr. Fenton, you'll have time to ride with me."

"Why don't you start riding it right now?" Papa asked. "Mama says you know how."

"You can ride over and show Gracie," Mama suggested.

Even in my excitement over the new wheel, I knew they were trying to get rid of me. But I didn't care. Showing off my new bicycle was what I wanted to do more than anything in the world.

I had outgrown taking dolls to bed with me but I occasionally sneaked a special treasure under my pillow. The last had been a pair of plaid stockings Mrs. Antha had given me for Easter. But that night I boldly wheeled the bicycle into my room and propped it by my bed. I didn't care whether or not Papa and Mama laughed.

It was still very hot and I kept waking up through the night with perspiration dampening my face. Each time I reached over and touched the cool frame of my gem. The handle bars were lacquered with moonlight. The bicycle was beautiful even in the half-darkness.

I, Helene Bradford, had a bicycle. And I was glad that Papa, instead of Mr. Fenton or even God, had given it to me.

* * *

About ten days after this, the baggage man at the railroad station sent word to the house that he had a crate down there for Mama. I rode down on my wheel to investigate. Through the slats I could see what it was: a bicycle for Mama! Grandfather's name, Ruthven Merriam, was written on a tag as the sender. Would wonders never cease in this very exciting summer?

When I got home, Mama already knew the surprise. Papa had brought the mail and there was a letter from Grandfather.

"Isn't it wonderful!" Mama cried. "Sit down and cool off, Helene. I want you to hear your grandfather's letter. He's such a smart man. I think his letters are part of our education."

She started reading:

August 1st, 1900

DEAR DAUGHTER,

I hope you like your new bicycle. I have been thinking of sending you one for some time as I feel that pedaling will be a healthful form of exercise for you. Lately I read that a new hygienic seat had been invented for bicycles. I found that the dealer had one of that type so I bought it.

Some old fogies have been preaching from pulpits that the bicycles will take girls away from their homes and away from proper chaperonage. That is one of the reasons I never go to church. I don't care to hear the gospel of the bicycle expounded.

I believe in freedom for women. You can ride your wheel

145

any place you please, but Helene is really just a little girl.
I thought it would be better to have you accompany her if
she wanted to ride on the country roads. She will soon
exhaust the possibilities of the two streets in Tory.

If I were to start bicycling, I would probably acquire some
new bumps on my head. I feel I don't need any new ones.
A phrenologist tried to read the ones I already have. The
man — he was a quack, I'm convinced — said I was not con-
sistent and I'd better start to reform. I said, "A foolish
consistency is the hobgoblin of little minds." Then I threw
the dollar I owed him on the table and walked out. I wanted
him to explain the principles of this so-called science. I
didn't care to have him make suggestions about my char-
acter. I'm too old to reform, but you're not.

I'm glad Frank bought the bicycle for Helene even if he
did take the money out of his savings. It's nice to have an
umbrella for any rainy day which might come to you, but
it's nicer for Helene to have a bicycle. You can see I'm not
consistent for I believe in saving, or at least I did when I
was young, although I'll never forgive myself for not buy-
ing your mother the Brussels carpet she wanted for the back
sitting room. But maybe it's just as well I did save. I am
living on the money I earned and saved when I had the
carriage-manufacturing company. I loan out money to peo-
ple who aren't as smart as I am.

Your obedient servant,

RUTHVEN R. MERRIAM

"Wasn't that a good letter?" Mama asked when she'd
finished. I nodded.

"And wasn't it sweet of him to give me the bicycle?"
Mama went on. "It's a highlight of my life. We'll have

so much fun together when we go riding. Someday I'm
going to have a real bicycle skirt."

Both of us did love our bicycles. Mama had quite a
hard time learning to ride. At first Papa, or Mr. Fenton,
or Uncle Will, whoever happened to be at the house,
had to walk beside her and hold her up. After she
learned to balance and stay on, other people on bicycles
had a fatal fascination for her. She couldn't seem to help
running into them. One day, Aunt Fan, Mama's rich
friend from Springfield, brought her bicycle out on the
B. and O. to surprise Mama. Her plan was that they
would go cycling together. Papa and I were at the house
when Aunt Fan got there. Mama had gone up on her
wheel to call on Mrs. Huddleston, Wilbur Newlin's
sister.

"Kate's gone north," Papa told Aunt Fan, "but if you
value your neck, you'd better ride south. She'll run into
you and knock you flat." Aunt Fan laughed and headed
north. But she did come home with dust on her divided
skirt.

"I guess," Papa said to me when Aunt Fan started out
to find Mama, "that I gave Fan pretty good advice.
When your mother's heading north, it's better to head
south. I should tell this to Wint Fenton, but I won't."

"I don't understand what you mean," I said.

"Not a thing. You know what Mrs. Blankenbarger said
about me, that I had more jokes than pills." He thought
a minute. "I'm wondering if the bicycle will help Kate

to feel that her layer of the lemon jelly cake has become a little bigger and better."

"What?" I asked again.

"Just another joke, honey," Papa said. "I guess I'm no Artemus Ward or Mr. Dooley when my jokes have to be labeled as such."

ELEVEN

THE FIRST SUNDAY IN AUGUST, GRACIE AND I were sitting in the hammock in our yard reading Elsie Dinsmore books. We'd read the whole series through once so now we took anyone that was handed to us at the Sunday School library. Gracie couldn't read anything else on Sunday, or ride her bicycle or play games, even Authors. She was my best friend so I didn't do these things either. We were tired of the Elsie books but they were a part of Sunday like wearing your best dress to Sunday School, eating fried chicken for dinner, feeling drowsy, having the bees buzz louder than on any other day, going over in the late afternoon to Mrs. Antha's to eat homemade ice cream, and waiting for the day to end so it would be Monday and you could start doing things again. It was such a bore to have a day of rest when you were never tired.

"Do you feel that romance is in the air?" Gracie asked.

"Is that in your book?" I wanted to know.

"Not on your tintype," Gracie said. "I was just thinking of something Mama said."

"What?" I asked.

149

"It was about Mr. Fenton. Don't you think he's romantic?"

"Oh yes," I agreed. "Isn't it a shame we're both too little to marry him? But it wouldn't do us any good. I don't know whether he'll ever come down any more."

"What do you mean?"

"Nothing," I said.

"You've got to tell me what's happened," Gracie said.

I had been frightened by Mama's crying when she said Mr. Fenton couldn't come down again. I could never stand to see Mama in tears. I wasn't going to tell Gracie about it. "He's too busy. Papa and Mama both said so." I felt I had to tell a lie.

This seemed to satisfy her. "Anyway there's romance in the air at summer resorts. It said so in one of Mama's magazines. Wouldn't you just love to go to a summer resort and wear a tennis dress?"

"And a bathing suit," I added. "I'll get a magazine and show you some pictures of bathing suits." I went into the house and brought out a June *Vogue* that Aunt Fan had brought to Mama.

"If anyone comes along, we can sit on the magazine," Gracie said. "Papa'd have a fit if he found me looking at a fashion book on Sunday."

I opened the magazine to the page which showed three bathing beauties. The hammock swayed as we studied them.

"I'll take this one," Gracie pointed to one of the

150

sketches. It showed a young woman in a dark bathing
suit reaching below her knees. With this she wore long
black stockings, and shoes which laced around her
ankles. On her head was a plaid tam.

This was a favorite game of ours, picking out cos-
tumes from magazines. We usually initialed them, and
then they were ours as much as if they were hanging
in our closets. I didn't mind having her choose first for
I liked the suit that was made of white serge with a
large collar and vestee much better. A cap with a bill
went with this outfit.

"The other suit can belong to Miss Rose," Gracie
said. We often liked to include Miss Rose, our Sunday
School teacher, in our fantasy world.

"Where would she wear it?" I asked.

"Don't be silly. She could wear it the same place we're
going to wear ours, which is no place," Gracie said.

"But we've already decided we're going to grow up
and marry rich husbands. They'll take us off to summer resorts, Newport, and every place. They'll have
to be from away."

"We sure don't want to marry Barbed-Wire Ernie or
Fat Snodgrass, or any of those boys in our room at
school," Gracie said.

"Especially Barbed-Wire Ernie," I said. "He's been so
stuck-up since he started going to the Springfield den-
tist and having those barbed wires put on his teeth."

"He sure thinks he's something," Gracie agreed.

"There might be romance in the air, right here in Tory." Gracie's idea had appealed to me. "If there is, maybe we could get it working on Miss Rose."

"But she's old," Gracie protested.

"Sometimes old people get married and get babies," I answered. "There was a story on the inside of the paper that told about a woman like that. Didn't you see it? It was just above the story about the chicken in South America that laid three eggs in one day. Of course, Papa said he doesn't believe all those things in the patent insides."

"Whose insides?" Gracie asked.

"Oh that's just what they call the inside of the paper," I said. "Little towns like Tory don't have enough exciting things happening so the papers, like *The Tory Item,* buy them and just add them to the rest of the stuff that does happen here, like people dying and getting married and going to spend the day with each other. Papa told me."

"I don't see why your father wouldn't believe things if they're in the papers," Gracie said.

I didn't understand it myself.

"Say!" Gracie sat up straight. "How about Homer Gillen? We could work on a romance for him and Miss Rose."

"No!" I stopped the hammock with my foot. "His wife hasn't been dead any time at all, he's got those five children and lives in that hot little house."

"He does smoke cigars," Gracie said. "Miss Rose wouldn't like that. You know she's always giving us Sunday School lessons on the evils of tobacco."

"But she likes Papa. He and Mr. Fenton smoke pipes," I said.

"But they aren't Christians," Gracie said.

"You mean they don't belong to any church." I struggled to keep my temper.

It was a sore subject with me. Gracie and I had discussed it many times. Mama didn't like it either. She said Papa was the finest Christian she knew.

Papa laughed when we got mad about it. He said there was a real reason and a good reason for doing everything. The good reason was the one you usually told people. His good reason for not being a church member in Tory was that he was a doctor and kept office hours on Sunday mornings. Since almost everybody in Tory went to church, he rarely had a patient, but he always went down to the office. That was when he caught up on his farm reading. He said his devotionals were intoning the articles in *The Prairie Farmer*. When he came home for Sunday dinner, he almost always had a new plan for a fruit farm drawn on the back of an envelope or else an estimate of how many quarts of currants could be raised on half an acre. When I had asked him his real reason for not being a church member he said it was because he didn't like to play the harp and that he liked derby hats better than halos.

Miss Rose must have had both a good reason and
a real reason for going to church. The church was her
whole life, Mr. Baldwin said. She had started teaching
Gracie and me in Sunday School when we were in the
infant class. As we moved into other departments she
moved with us. She said she couldn't give up her little
girls. She called us her sunbeams.

Papa called Miss Rose Neal one of the left-behind
women. She had belonged to a big family and had been
brought up on a farm. The rest of the family married.
When the father died, Miss Rose and her mother moved
into Tory. Mrs. Neal was now old and partially para-
lyzed. Naturally it fell to Miss Rose's lot to take care of
her. She was a cross old woman who always pounded
with her cane for attention every time Gracie and I
were there calling on Miss Rose.

Mama called her poor Miss Rose. She often asked her
for supper when Papa was on a baby case. I'd go after
her. On the way over she'd tell me how sweet and pretty
Mama was. Most of the married women in the village
didn't have any use for Miss Rose because she'd done
the Terrible Thing. But Mama was sweet, just as Miss
Rose said. She never made any fuss over the Terrible
Thing.

The Terrible Thing was the burning of the feathers
in a featherbed so she could use the ticking to make a
petticoat. Feathers were terribly expensive. Ticking
petticoats were fashionable. The Neals didn't have any

154

money to buy ticking so once when the family was away she had burned up the feathers in a big feather-bed and had washed and cut the ticking into a petticoat before the family got home. Most people thought Miss Rose didn't get married because she'd done the Terrible Thing, although Mrs. Antha insisted she didn't get married because she had lumps in her gravy.

I didn't think Gracie would know, either, whether it was the feathers or the lumps that had kept her single. She was still busy studying the fashion book.

"I know what we can do for Miss Rose and romance," I said. "We can get Brother Wilbur interested in her. After all, he's one of our best friends."

"Why didn't we think of that before?" Gracie dropped the magazine in her excitement. "Do you suppose Miss Rose ever thought of him as a beau?"

"I don't think Miss Rose ever thinks of beaux," I said.

"She should," Gracie says. "Heck, Mama says every woman wants to get married."

"Maybe Miss Rose just thinks of him as a lovable child. Mama says that's the way people treat Wilbur, even Mrs. Huddleston. But Papa's going to get him to make a band for the eagle. That shows he trusts him," I said.

"The eagle?" Gracie asked.

"I wasn't supposed to tell about that," I said.

"You've got to tell me. You never did have secrets

from me until today," Gracie said with some concern.

"But you're not going to be in town next week when they let the eagle go," I said.

"You mean your father's really got an eagle, a live eagle? They steal children, and fly away with them," Gracie said.

"I know. I guess that's why Papa's got it in a coop in the shed back of his office. A patient brought it in to him. Wilbur's going to make the band for its leg and they're going to have an eagle-freeing ceremony. They weren't going to ask anybody but I'll get them to ask Miss Rose. Then I can throw her and Wilbur together," I said.

"You can tell them that — "

"I know what I'll say. I'll say to Wilbur that Miss Rose thinks his leg band is just wonderful and that she doesn't have lumps in her gravy any more. I didn't think she had too many lumps the time she had us for supper, did you?"

"No, it was good," Gracie said. "You can say — "

"I'm working it out," I interrupted Gracie again. "I'll tell Miss Rose that Wilbur admires people who give themselves to their church. I need you for that part but I guess I can handle it alone."

"I'm just sick I have to go to Peoria next week and visit Papa's cousins," Gracie said. "Why are they making the band for the eagle's leg?"

"Eagles live for just centuries. But sometime it will

156

die, maybe in Africa or Asia. The band's going to have
Papa's and Wilbur's names on it, and where they live.
Then people who find the dead eagle can write and — "

"But if that's hundreds of years off, you'll all be dead.
You'll just have to get married and have descendants,"
Gracie said.

"Oh, I'm going to get married," I said firmly. "I'm
never going to let the skin get tight on my face like
Miss Rose's or wear frizzy bangs."

Just then Papa drove up. He hitched Mike in front.
That meant he'd have to make another call after supper.

"I must go." Gracie got up from the hammock. It was
late.

I walked to the gate with Gracie, then I hurried into
the house to start working on Papa and Mama to invite
Miss Rose to the eagle ceremony.

They were sitting in the front room talking when I
came in. I didn't waste any time starting on my romantic
project. "There's somebody, somebody special, I wish
we could have the day we set the eagle free."

Nobody answered. Papa and Mama just sat there
looking at each other.

Finally Papa said, "I'd like to have him, too — and,
by Jesus, we'll have him."

"Him? I meant Miss Rose," I said.

"And I meant Wint Fenton," Papa said. I never saw
him more determined. "I'll write to Wint right now."
Papa got up and went to the walnut desk in the corner.

157

TWELVE

MR. FENTON WROTE BY RETURN MAIL THAT HE would be delighted to come to the eagle ceremony. It was to be on the following Friday because Wilbur wouldn't have the band for the eagle ready until then. In the meantime Papa read in the Springfield paper that the insurance case, the case that had been bringing him to Springfield, was to be tried in a Chicago court that same week.

Before Mama got upset about the bicycle, we'd had an arrangement with Mr. Fenton. He'd promised to let Mama know whenever he had business in Springfield. That way, Mama could invite him to Tory. Mr. Fenton wasn't the kind who'd come without an invitation.

Papa was sure Mr. Fenton would have to stay in Chicago for the hearing. Still, he hadn't telegraphed that he couldn't come. It would be exciting to get a telegram but more fun, I thought, to have him here. I rode my bike down to the morning train, hoping he'd get off.

He did.

When we got to the house, Mama was sitting on the

158

little porch in her new pink dimity. Mrs. Antha had given her the material. She said she'd had the piece goods laying around the house so long she was sick of the sight of it.

"I never saw you in pink before," Mr. Fenton said.

"Mrs. Antha gave her the goods," I said.

"No detail is too small for Helene," Mama said.

I didn't care. Mr. Fenton knew all about us by this time. "Doesn't Mama look beautiful? I think she looks just like she stepped out of *The Rose Fairy Book*."

"Even prettier than that," Mr. Fenton said.

"Children!" Mama cried.

Mr. Fenton just laughed. He didn't seem to mind being called a child.

"Where did Frank get the eagle?" he asked.

"The eagle was stealing chickens on the Bass farm. They didn't know it was an eagle. They thought it was some kind of hawk. Mr. Bass shot at it. The shot must have stunned it, anyway it fell to the ground and Mr. Bass picked it up and put it in a chicken coop. Then he brought it to Frank."

"Was it to go on the doctor bill?" I asked.

"Of course not," said Mama. "It was a present. I've told you and told you not to talk about the bills."

"I'm sorry," I said hurriedly. I wanted to go on with the story. "Papa says eagles soar and he's going to see this one gets its chance in life. They're rare around here now. When the country used to be just for the Indians

159

he thinks there were lots of eagles. I guess Papa told you about the leg band."

"Yes, he told me in his letter," Mr. Fenton said. "The eagle is our native bird. I wouldn't have missed this patriotic ceremony for anything."

"Frank is having lots of fun with it," Mama said. "He doesn't have enough fun."

"There are other people who don't, either," Mr. Fenton said.

"You mean slum children?" I asked. "I read about them."

"I must have meant something like that," Mr. Fenton said.

"You'd better ride up and tell Papa Mr. Fenton is here," Mama turned to me.

The ceremony was in the early afternoon. Papa took the coop down in the buggy. There wasn't any room for the rest of us. He offered to come back for Mama and Mr. Fenton but we wanted to pick up Miss Rose so we all walked.

"We're having Miss Rose for a special reason," I said to Mr. Fenton as we walked along. "She's Gracie's and my Sunday School teacher. We think she should have a romance. Summer's the time for romance. She's real old, she must be almost forty. We don't want to let too many summers go by."

"Who's the lucky man?" Mr. Fenton asked.

160

"It's Wilbur Newlin. You know, up where we're going for the ceremony. He's making the eagle's leg band," I said.

"I remember him," Mr. Fenton said. "I met him at your party."

"We thought about you for Miss Rose," I said. "But I said she wasn't pretty enough. You wouldn't want to marry anybody who wasn't pretty, would you?"

"Helene!" Mama said.

"I guess I'm getting personal again," I said. "But I don't know how you can talk about persons without being personal."

"Go on," Mr. Fenton said. "How did you happen to decide on your friend Wilbur? Hasn't he known Miss Rose for a good many years?"

"Sort of," I said. "He comes to church with his sister, Mrs. Huddleston. Miss Rose is always there, too. But Gracie and I think he just looks at her as if she were one of the pews. Besides he has his mind on inventing, even in church. He's trying to think up some kind of horn Mr. Baldwin can talk through so everyone can hear him better."

"He's an interesting fellow," Mr. Fenton agreed. "I feel flattered to be the only guest besides Miss Rose."

"It was all Papa's idea to ask you," I said.

"Frank didn't want to have everybody in town come," Mama said. "It would give them another chance to laugh at Wilbur. They've made enough fun of Wilbur

161

already. He's always up to something unusual, something they don't understand. And even Antha and Will would think it 'plumb crazy' of Frank to band an eagle."

Miss Rose was ready when we stopped for her. It didn't take long to walk the rest of the way. When we got there, Mrs. Huddleston came out and shook hands. She seemed pleased Papa had asked Wilbur to help. Papa and the eagle had already arrived. He and Wilbur and a man from the farm were bending over the coop trying to fasten the band on the eagle's leg.

"It's tame from being shut up so long so don't worry," Papa called to us. "It won't attack any of you."

Mrs. Huddleston lived on a farm that adjoined the village. Her husband had built a beautiful big house just before he died. It had a bay window, a cupola, and a porch that ran around two sides. The porch was narrow so Mrs. Huddleston and Wilbur always sat out in the back yard when they wanted to be outdoors. There was a big grassy space here with a vegetable garden at the back. Near this was Wilbur's inventing shed. The grounds ran down to a little stream where they cut the ice in winter. An ice house stood on the bank.

Wilbur had brought out extra chairs for us to sit on while we watched the ceremony. There was a palm-leaf fan on every chair.

Mrs. Huddleston was a small dark woman. She had always worn black since her husband died, even in the summer. She wasn't very pretty except when she smiled at Wilbur. Wilbur didn't have any other family and he'd always lived with the Huddlestons. Today Mrs. Huddleston had on a thin black voile. Miss Rose wore brown. It was her year-before-last's best dress. I was mad at her because she wasn't more dressed-up. Even her best foot, which Papa said she never put forward, had on an ugly black shoe. Mama's new pink dress looked beautiful against the bright green grass. When she walked around it swished. Canary said she liked to iron Mama's ruffled, lace-trimmed petticoats. Even if Mama didn't have many new dresses she always had plenty of those.

We all sat and talked until finally the band was fastened on the eagle's leg. Then Wilbur and the hired man carried the coop out on the lawn some distance in front of us. Papa stood up by it. "I am going to make a speech," he announced. "We have here before us an eagle, a noble example of the *Aquila chrysaëtus.* As you know, the eagle is our native bird, chosen by our forefathers to represent us, just as the lion represents England and the bear, Russia. It has been a proper symbol. We have flown high and nobly since we have been a nation, more than fourscore and seven years ago."

Mr. Fenton clapped and we all joined in.

Papa bowed and went on. "How this noble eagle, this glorious bird, happened to be in Tory, Illinois, I do not know. But we have had many distinguished visitors this summer. My first thought when the bird was given to me was to free it and let it soar majestically away. Then I thought of Wilbur Newlin, one of the smartest men in Tory."

I was pleased about this. Papa was playing right into my hands, showing Wilbur off before Miss Rose.

"I decided to ask Wilbur to help me on what I thought would be an interesting experiment," Papa continued. "We would band the eagle before we set it free. Wilbur made the band of copper. He made a key to lock the band on. This key will be put in a box in the Tory State Bank, an institution which I am sure will be here long after we are gone. Wilbur took his engraving tool and inscribed his name and mine on the band, along with our address and the date. To this he added the instructions to notify us if the eagle is ever found again. The eagle is a long-lived bird. Even the most learned scholars do not know how long eagles live. Nor do we know just where the majestic wings of our mighty friend will carry him — perhaps to Tanganyika, Vladivostok, Tierra del Fuego or Samarkand," Papa said. I didn't know whether all those places were real, or whether Papa was just making them up. I'd never heard him make a speech before.

"Let the eagle soar! And let our imaginations soar with it! May it know ten full decades of this glorious new century! May it know the feel of the icy Siberian winds against its wings, the soothing perfume of the

164

Hawaiian lotus. From our continent, our century, may it sweep on to other continents, other centuries!" Papa finished with a broad swing of his right hand. His forehead glistened in the sunlight.

"Frank should be a politician," Mr. Fenton whispered to Mama. "I never heard a better speech."

"And now," Papa took hold of the coop, "we free you, our American eagle! We who are earthbound envy you!"

Wilbur and the hired man opened one side of the coop. But the eagle didn't move.

"I'll go after him with a broomstick." Wilbur ran to the inventing shed and picked up a broom which was standing by the door. He came back and poked at the eagle. At last it stepped out on the grass. Miss Rose gave a nice feminine little scream. The eagle stood blinking for a few minutes, then it flew to a plum tree near the vegetable garden.

"Let's get the clothes prop and get it out of there," Papa said to Wilbur. It took several pokes before the eagle moved. Finally it flew. Rising above the little stream it disappeared over the walnut grove beyond. We all clapped and clapped.

"That was a great speech, Doc," Wilbur said.

"It was wonderful," Mama said.

"I could hardly keep from crying." Miss Rose got out her handkerchief and wiped her eyes.

"I thought we ought to have a little fun out of it."

Papa winked at Mr. Fenton. "I didn't know you girls would take me so seriously. But, by Jesus, I meant most of it."

"Did you make that speech up right out of your head, Doc?" Wilbur asked.

"You sounded almost as good as Mr. Baldwin," Miss Rose said.

"Better!" I cried. "Do you suppose the eagle's on his way to Asia or Africa?"

"I wouldn't be at all surprised," Papa said.

"I've made some lemonade," Mrs. Huddleston said. "Wilbur, you can help me carry it out."

"Why don't you go, too?" I suggested to Miss Rose. "You can see how Wilbur can put things on the tray. He's so helpful. He helps keep the house as neat as a pin."

Wilbur came back first with a table from the porch. Then he brought out the big tray filled with glasses. Mrs. Huddleston followed with the pitcher of lemonade and Miss Rose carried a big china chop plate filled with coconut cookies and small jam cakes.

We all ate and drank and talked about the eagle. Then I suggested that we go look at the inventing shed. It wasn't very big but I crowded in first with Wilbur so I could help explain things.

"These are for the clock that's going to run backwards," I said, pointing to a row of clocks, most of them with parts missing. "It's to time horse races because

166

they run counter-clockwise." Then I realized this was
bad since Miss Rose wouldn't approve of horse racing.
Wilbur loved racing but only Gracie and I knew about
that. "It's for other people than us," I added. "All inventions are."

"And these are parts for the gold panner," I moved
over to a long table by the wall. "It's to pan fool's gold
out of coal."

"How interesting," Mr. Fenton said. He studied some
drawings pinned on the wall. "I see you're turning your
hand to a lot of things."

Miss Rose was acting like a ninny, a perfect ninny.
She just stood there and didn't say a word.

"Wilbur's going to make a fortune some day out of
his inventions," I said.

"Oh, I wouldn't say that," Wilbur said.

Then everybody walked out to look at Mrs. Huddleston's garden. I fell behind with Wilbur. "Don't you
think Miss Rose is sweet?" I asked.

Wilbur didn't answer. He rarely had much to say
except to Gracie and me when we were helping him
invent.

"I don't think it was bad for her to burn up those
feathers just because she wanted to make a petticoat,
do you?" I continued.

"Nope," Wilbur said.

"She makes the best gravy, no lumps at all. I've had
it at her house," I said. Wilbur paid no attention to this

so I decided maybe he hadn't heard what Mrs. Antha thought about her gravy.

Shortly after that it was time to go home. Papa drove Mama and Mr. Fenton in the buggy.

"Wilbur can walk home with Miss Rose and me," I said.

"Wilbur?" Miss Rose asked in just the dumbest way.

"It's not dark," Wilbur said.

"But you always take Gracie and me a piece when we're going home," I said.

"All right," Wilbur agreed.

The walks were narrow. I fell behind. Wilbur wasn't saying a thing. I wished he'd watch Mr. Fenton to see how he acted with women. We came to the corner where I had to turn off. Miss Rose suggested that Wilbur go with me. "Oh no," I said. "I'm going to hustle." I ran the length of two lots, then I stopped and looked back at Miss Rose and Wilbur. Maybe when they were alone, Miss Rose would talk and be sweet.

She knew such good stories. Last week at Sunday School she had told us about a little boy who went skating on Sunday and was drowned. The week before our lesson was on greediness. Miss Rose knew just the story for this. It was about a little girl in Easton, Pennsylvania, who was too stingy to put her pennies in the collection box. On the way home she was counting her money and didn't see a runaway horse that came charging down upon her. She was knocked flat and severely

168

injured. Mrs. Baldwin said Miss Rose got these stories out of the *Sunday School Teachers' Journal.* But I didn't believe that; Miss Rose always told the stories as if she knew the people.

I hoped people would see Wilbur and Miss Rose together and they might begin to say Miss Rose had a beau. Mama always said nothing succeeded like success.

When I got home Mama and Papa and Mr. Fenton were sitting in the front room talking.

"I don't see why you and Frank can't come to Chicago and visit me," Mr. Fenton said. "I've made so many visits here."

"We didn't know whether you'd come this time on account of the insurance case," I said.

Mr. Fenton turned to me. "I would think anybody who could diagnose Mrs. Blankenbarger could also diagnose my case — I really come down to see the Bradfords, not the men in the State House."

Mama looked uncomfortable, the way she looked when Gracie and I sang duets.

"Couldn't you come up?" Mr. Fenton said.

"Oh no," Mama said.

"Maybe — " Papa hesitated. "Maybe in September, when Helene is back in school. I might be too busy — but Kate must come."

Just then Spider Benson knocked on the door. Papa opened it. "Doc," he said, "I just shot down a big bird, over there beyond Mrs. Huddleston's grove. I thought it was a chicken hawk but it had a funny thing on its leg saying to notify either you or Wilbur Newlin. What'll I do with it?"

"The eagle!" Mama cried. We just sat there looking at each other.

"I don't give a good God damn," Papa said.

"I didn't mean to," Spider said.

"I know you didn't," Papa said. He took fifty cents out of his pocket and gave it to Spider. "Here, you take this and get rid of that bird some way. I never want to see it again."

None of us said a word. It was too sad. I felt as if we'd had a death in the family.

"See?" Papa said to Mr. Fenton. "I get to soaring too high, then something like this happens. No, Kate will go alone to Chicago."

I tried to think up something to say but I couldn't. I didn't know whether I was sorrier for Papa or the eagle.

THIRTEEN

THE NEXT MORNING, MAMA, MR. FENTON, AND I took turns riding on the bicycles. Mr. Fenton looked funny on a woman's bike, with his long legs almost hitting the handle bars. But we had fun.

"I don't see how you manage so well on the dirt road," he told Mama. "When I hit a clod of dirt, I almost take a tumble. You should come up to Chicago sometime and ride on the smooth pavements."

"I'd never get there on a bicycle," Mama said.

"I could rent one for you," Mr. Fenton said.

"That would be silly when there's so much to see and do in the city," Mama said.

"Frank said you could come," Mr. Fenton said.

"I'd have to give it a lot of thought," Mama said. "I'm still in my layer of the lemon jelly cake."

"But a trip to Chicago could be the lemon jelly on the layer," Mr. Fenton said.

No one had suggested that I go to Chicago, too. I didn't understand it when Mama was always saying I should have advantages.

"Isn't it almost train time?" Mama asked.

171

"Let's ride to the station," I suggested.

"You can, but Mr. Fenton has his bag to carry," Mama said. "We'll walk."

At the station, Mr. Fenton kissed me good-by. He always did but he'd never kissed Mama since the very first time he'd left. I asked Papa about it once and he said he guessed Mr. Fenton must have been swept off his feet by Mama's beauty. Then he added, "I'm just being foolish. I'm sure he kissed her because we were all perfect strangers to him then and he felt he owed Mama something for being so nice to him and having him for supper. Your Mama does lots of nice things for people."

When we got home from the train, Mama unloosened the high collar on her blue gingham dress and we sat down on the little front porch to rest a minute.

"Mr. Fenton said you told him this summer was like a string of beads."

I nodded, suddenly self-conscious.

"I told him I thought this summer was like a meadow full of daisies. You picked them and picked and more grew in their place," Mama said.

"Especially if you give bunches of them away," I suggested. "Papa says you are always giving people things, like baby clothes and cookies, and that you're always doing nice things for people."

"Why, that's sweet of Frank to say that," Mama said.

172

"What did Mr. Fenton say this summer was like?" I asked, knowing he always had ideas on all subjects.

"A bolt of lightning," Mama said.

"He meant because we have thunderstorms?" I asked.

"I suppose so," Mama answered.

"I'm not going to have the days like beads any more," I said.

"Why not?" Mama asked.

"Oh I'm just tired of thinking about that," I said. "You know poets don't write all their poems just alike. I don't think I had very good luck with Miss Rose and Brother Wilbur. They could have been beads."

"I suspected that yesterday," Mama said.

"Poor Miss Rose," I went on.

"Oh, I don't know," Mama hesitated. "She never has any emotional problems."

"What does that mean?"

"Things you can't settle by looking them up in a book," Mama said. "And that makes me think, I have Mrs. Antha's new church cook book over here. Let's look up the recipe for that new dish, Cheese Fondu. Frank loves cheese. We can make it for dinner."

We went into the kitchen. I opened the book. "Oh look! Here in the back it has a recipe for cooking husbands." I began reading snatches aloud, " 'Some women go about it as if their husbands were bladders and blow them up; others keep them constantly in hot water; others roast them; some keep them in a pickle all their

173

lives. . . . Do not go to market for a husband for the best are always brought to your door.'" I put down the book. "I guess that's what Gracie and I were trying to do for Miss Rose, going to market to get her a husband."

"I'm afraid so," Mama said.

"'Add a little sugar in the form of what confectioners call kisses,'" I read on. "Don't you think this recipe is funny?"

"Not very," Mama said.

"But Mrs. Antha does. She was reading it to Uncle Will and me just the other day."

"I know, dear, and we love Mrs. Antha, but everybody doesn't have the same tastes."

"You mean it's the same as the gilded rolling pins and the calendars from the grocery store? You don't like those things."

"Yes," Mama agreed.

"I want to think the same things you do are funny," I said.

"How everybody spoils me," Mama said.

"And who deserves it more?" Papa said, coming into the kitchen.

"You're early," Mama said. "I haven't put on one apron, let alone two."

The good housekeepers of Tory wore two aprons. The top one was usually a dark calico and the underneath one white. *If* anyone came to call the top apron

174

could be whisked off. In their white one they were all dressed up for company.

"Don't put on any apron," Papa said. "Let's have a loaf of bread beneath the bough. I mean the grape arbor."

"A flask of wine, a book of verse — and thou," Mama added.

My, but I had smart parents! I didn't care if the villagers said they were booky. "And we can have lemon jelly cake. There's some left," I suggested, remembering Mama's other talents. She didn't go around with her nose in a book all the time!

I was glad we had such a good time at noon.

In the afternoon Papa came home with very bad news. Canary was terribly sick.

"I'm going to take her in to the hospital in Springfield. I know it means an operation right away. You call Dr. Ryan and tell him we're coming." Papa was excited.

"I'm going along, too," Mama said. "Canary'll be frightened."

"Yes, that's a good idea," Papa said. He had never allowed Mama to go on any case and help with the nursing but this was special. "I'll go down after Canary. We'll have to drive in. I don't want to wait for the evening train."

"Helene, you can help me. Get out some things so

I can stay all night, while I telephone the doctor,"
Mama instructed me. "I love the Catholic sisters but
Canary might be afraid of their big headgear."

I went into the bedroom and dragged from the closet
the old telescope bag she used for trips. With her directions, I found her best muslin nightgown, the one Mrs.
Antha had made for her the Christmas before. I put
in the pink challis wrapper, which was put away for
best, and her knitted bedroom slippers. I found her
toothbrush and opened the can of toothpowder Papa
always made up for us and poured some in an envelope.
"I'm going to send my violet perfume for Canary," I
said. "She loves flowers." This was one of my dearest
treasures. It came in a small, blue velvet wheelbarrow
with brass wheels, and had artificial violets tied to the
neck of the bottle.

"That's sweet of you," Mama said. "I'll tell Canary to
save the bottle and we can have it refilled someday.
And I think you'd better put in another dress for me,
my dark blue voile."

By this time, Papa was waiting outside. We both hurried out. Canary was sitting beside him, propped against
his shoulder. Her skin, usually such a warm brown, was
now gray; her lips were blue. She waved a feeble hand
at me.

Mama got in the buggy, drew Canary to her, and
gently rested Canary's head on her shoulder. She
turned to me, "Helene, you go over and stay with Antha

176

and Will until I get back. I was so excited I forgot to
make plans."

"But I'm going down to Gracie's for supper." I wasn't
invited often for a meal as Mrs. Baldwin hated to cook.

"Oh, yes," Mama answered. "You can go but you
can't stay all night. Remember! Go to Mrs. Antha's for
all night. Run over and tell them you are coming. You
can't sleep at the Baldwins'."

"Bedbugs?" I called after them.

Mama put her finger to her lips and looked ashamed
for me. Bedbugs was a word which was always whispered, and here I had screamed it at the top of my
lungs. Mama had never hinted such a thing about the
Baldwins, in fact she was always defending Mrs. Baldwin's untidiness by saying some women just weren't
born-housekeepers. I looked around. The only person
in sight was Spider Benson busily cutting the Joneses'
hedge. Fortunately he was a little deaf.

On the way down to the Baldwins', I remembered
that the quilting society had met that day at the church.
They brought their own lunch and gave what was left
to the Baldwins. Gracie was always bragging about the
good things that fell to their lot. When she'd invited
me, she had said something about eating scraps.

I often went over to Mrs. Antha's to eat what she
called scraps. Her scraps this time of year were usually
a platter of cold fried chicken, the leftover mashed
potatoes made into cakes and fried until crusty, corn

177

cut from the cob, mixed with lima beans and drifting in butter, and an open-faced pie. Mrs. Antha didn't trust herself to make as small an amount of crust as it took for a one-crust pie, so if they got hungry for lemon, custard or cream pie, she always made two. Then I was either invited over for supper or the extra pie was sent intact to our house.

But the scraps at the Baldwins' really lived up to their name. When I arrived, the food from the quilting luncheon had been put on the dining room table and covered with an extra tablecloth. A ketchup bottle in the center held this up like a tent.

The Baldwins usually ate in the kitchen, and the unused dining room table held an assortment of odds and ends, letters, papers, bits of sewing, an empty box or two. In the fruit dish in the center were buttons, hooks and eyes, tacks, screws, a couple of small empty bottles and occasionally a penny. But on the days when any of the church societies were meeting at the church next door, Mrs. Baldwin swept the clutter into a drawer and hid the fruit dish for some women always made an excuse to come over to the parsonage.

Today, Mrs. Baldwin was dressed in a black wool skirt and a white shirtwaist with a lace yoke. She had been dressed-up all day because of the quilting. After I arrived, she went into the kitchen to make coffee and finally called us to supper.

We took our places and because I was the guest

178

Gracie was asked to say grace. It was a verse her father had taught her. He had come from the Pennsylvania Dutch country and had said it as a child. Gracie bowed her head and recited it.

> I must not leave upon my plate
> The crust I cannot eat,
> For many a little hungry one
> Would think it quite a treat.
> My parents labor very hard
> To give me wholesome food,
> And I must not waste a bit
> That would do others good.
> For willful waste makes woeful want,
> And I might live to say,
> "Oh how I wish I had that crust
> That once I threw away."

Gracie never had anything to willfully waste, I thought, as I looked at the food. There were two dishes of potato salad, a glass bowl of pickled beets, another of cottage cheese which I imagined had been brought by Mrs. Blankenbarger because it was yellow with cream. In the center was a platter of fried chicken and a few slices of ham.

"You little girls can have the wings. I like the ham best," Mr. Baldwin said, helping himself to a piece.

When the platter came around to Mrs. Baldwin, she picked at it with her fork. "Just backs," she said bitterly.

"Now, Effie, I bet you had some good pieces of breast for dinner," Mr. Baldwin said.

179

"I sure did," she answered. "Two of them."

"We can fill up on cake." Gracie eyed the heaped-up plate at one end of the table.

"Lots of people brought cake today. Be sure and eat the banana, it won't keep," Mrs. Baldwin answered. The slices of banana on the frosting were already beginning to turn dark. I knew Papa and Mama were always sorry for the Baldwins so I took a piece of it, even though it didn't look good to me.

"You can have another piece, too," Mr. Baldwin said.

"No thank you," I answered. I'd had a large piece of lemon jelly cake before I'd left home.

"Your mother didn't come to the quilting," Mrs. Baldwin said.

"No. Mr. Fenton was there."

"Oh," Mrs. Baldwin said. There was a silence.

"He came to see me this morning," Mr. Baldwin volunteered.

"What did he want?" Mrs. Baldwin demanded.

"He left me some money to buy a tombstone for Harry Simpson." Mr. Baldwin took a piece of paper out of his pocket. I could see Mr. Fenton had used some of Mama's light blue writing paper. "He wants to have this inscribed on it. 'Know then thyself, presume,'" Mr. Baldwin stumbled a little over the word, "'not God to scan; the proper study of mankind is man [Pope].' He said Harry Simpson taught him a lot."

"Pope was a poet," I said. "Mama says so." I didn't want them to keep on discussing Mr. Fenton.

"I wish I had time to sit around and read poetry like your mama does," Mrs. Baldwin commented.

I was tempted to say, "But Mama's a good manager." This was true because Papa said so, Mrs. Antha did and Mama even admitted it herself. Feeling just like Elsie Dinsmore who always turned the other cheek, I kept still. Oh dear, if I were only as pretty as Elsie!

Then on the other cheek landed Mrs. Baldwin's next remark, "I wonder what your mother's going to do about her washing now that Canary is sick?"

"I don't know," I answered. I *was* Elsie Dinsmore!

After supper, Mr. Baldwin, Gracie, and I went into his study and played parchesi. Mr. Fenton had given Gracie and me each a board for the game and since it wasn't cards it was perfectly all right for the Baldwins to play.

Mama and Papa played whist and euchre. Mama had even gone in to a bid-euchre party Aunt Fan had given in Springfield and won the lone-hand prize, a small glass smelling salts bottle with a silver top. Mama wasn't the fainting kind and didn't need smelling salts but she loved the little bottle and kept it on her bureau. It was so much nicer to be married to a doctor than a minister, and be able to win prizes.

While we were playing, Mrs. Baldwin went out and

181

took a walk. She wasn't even home when it was time for Mr. Baldwin and Gracie to walk up to Mrs. Antha's with me.

I thought it was strange and mentioned it to Uncle Will and Mrs. Antha. "Sam Blankenbarger's been playing checkers with me all evening up at the store," Uncle Will said.

"Will!" Mrs. Antha shook her head at him and then nodded in my direction. "I didn't finish making up your bed, Helene," she hastened to add, "I didn't know whether you'd rather have the wedding ring quilt or the log cabin or the rose of Sharon or the red, white, and blue or — "

"The log cabin. I like all the little straight pieces. Because it's neat," I answered. I was thinking of the Baldwin house.

"That's a funny reason to like a quilt," she replied. "But come on, you've got to get to bed. Your eyes are just like burnt holes in a blanket."

The next morning when I woke up I could hear Papa's voice downstairs. I jumped out of bed and ran downstairs in my nightgown. Papa was sitting at the kitchen table eating breakfast.

"How's Canary?" I threw my arms around Papa.

"She got along fine but I left your mother at the hospital with her for the night. I got home before midnight. I was glad I took Kate." Papa turned to the Joneses. "She went right in the operating room with

182

Canary and held her hand until she went under the
chloroform. Canary was frightened. When she came to
she said she'd have died of fright if it hadn't been for
Kate. I had them put up a cot in the room. But Kate's
coming home today, honey." Papa reached over and
patted my hand.

"Goody," I cried. "I thought maybe she'd have to
stay all the time."

"That's why you looked so worried last night," Mrs.
Antha said.

"I didn't have a very good time at the Baldwins,"
I said. "But I shouldn't say that. Gracie's my best
friend."

"She misses her Mama," Uncle Will said. "We all do.
But you just pull up a chair by Uncle Will and start
putting your teeth into some of these batter cakes.
Here, let Uncle Will cut them up and pour on the
sorghum."

"Don't give her those cold cakes, Will. The very
idea," Mrs. Antha jumped up to pour more batter on
the griddle. I could see them getting bubbly and crisp
around the edges.

"My turn next," Papa said.

"Don't forget to leave room for fresh fried cakes,"
Uncle Will said.

"You've made doughnuts!" I cried.

"Sure," Mrs. Antha answered. "I don't often get
Frank over here for breakfast. I'd have called you to

183

help fry the little balls out of the centers, Helene, but you were sleeping so pretty."

"We have the best neighbors in the world," Papa said.

"You didn't think I'd let a man try to get his own breakfast?" Mrs. Antha asked.

"If Mama were only here," I said, as I took my first bite of the hot pancakes.

And Papa said, "We miss her."

FOURTEEN

CANARY'S OPERATION WAS ONE OF THE BIGGEST events that ever happened in Tory. For the first few days, our telephone rang constantly for news. Everyone loved Canary. There were few homes where she hadn't helped. She seemed to be part of everybody's family. Mrs. Antha started a fund to pay for the operation and her hospital expenses. She and Uncle Will headed the list with the sum of $25.00 written after their names. The first person she called on was Minnie Overstreet who immediately signed up for a like sum. The Blankenbargers gave the same amount. From there on the sums dropped to a smaller figure but everybody seemed eager to contribute. Gracie even offered to sell her parchesi board so she would have money to give. But when Mrs. Antha heard of this she hired her, and me, to pick plums, and when we came in with a bushel basketful she added fifty cents in each of our names to the collection.

"If they're not careful," Papa said, "they'll have enough money to pay for a statue to Canary. She already has one of the best rooms in the hospital."

"She's an institution in the village," Mama agreed.

"I don't know any better person. We've never had a hero here," Papa said.

"We've got Mr. Civil War," I said, remembering the statue Gracie and I had unveiled, which stood near the gate of the cemetery.

"Yes, but he isn't anybody," Papa said. "We just bought the statue because we'd been collecting money in the Horse-Thief treasury for years and didn't know what to do with it."

"Antihorse Thief," Mama corrected.

Papa laughed.

"You just don't say *anti* to tease me," Mama said.

"No, I just happen to live in Tory, Illinois. You know when you live in Rome. I wouldn't say Antihorse *Thief* any more than I'd call Antha Jones by her real name, Samantha. It's healthy to have some simple thing to quarrel about."

When Canary was better and could see visitors, the whole village wanted to go. But Papa said her company must be limited. This time, Minnie Overstreet had charge of a list. If anyone wanted to visit Canary, they had to consult this list and have a definite time assigned. Even Mrs. Antha agreed to this and humbly walked up to Minnie's and asked when she and Will could make their call.

"They'll be giving each other their secret recipes before long," Mama said.

186

"I wouldn't count on that," Papa answered. "I've seen too many deathbed scenes when everybody was repentant, then the patient recovered and the people fought as much as ever. Sometimes I've thought, by Jesus, I shouldn't be such a good doctor."

Because of the fund, Canary stayed in the hospital three weeks. Papa said she might as well get her strength back. At last the early September day approached when Canary was to be brought home. Fortunately for Gracie and me, school hadn't started since the repairs on the schoolhouse which had been started in July still weren't finished.

Mrs. Antha had announced at the beginning of the illness that she and Will would hitch up their team, take the surrey and bring her. This seemed to be accepted as the procedure, until word got around that Minnie Overstreet was planning to bring Canary home in a horseless carriage! Mrs. Overstreet didn't have a car. There were none in the village and none had ever passed through. But a man in Springfield had one which could be hired for rides and the gossip was that Minnie had rented it for the occasion.

Excitement whipped the village to a froth over this new development in the Antha Jones-Minnie Overstreet feud. Whom would Canary choose? The more conservative members of the community felt she would come in the surrey, the more daring ones were sure Canary wouldn't pass up a chance to ride in an auto-

187

mobile. Bets were laid by the men. Mrs. Neal and Mrs. Blankenbarger quarreled so bitterly over what would be Canary's decision that they didn't speak for six months.

Mrs. Antha was too proud to discuss the problem with anyone but us. "Minnie's just doing this to show off," she said. "She don't want to ride in one of these new-fangled things. Inside she'll be scared skinny. But she can't stand it because Will has that fancy team of blacks and everybody took it for granted we'd bring Canary. It isn't safe for Canary to ride in such a contraption! She'll bust her stitches wide open. I'd think you wouldn't allow it, Frank!"

"I don't think it would hurt her," Papa said. "I'm just Canary's doctor. I can't mix up in her transportation problems."

"You're as bad as Canary, Frank." Mrs. Antha was disgusted. "You never do speak your mind. Everybody that's been in to see Canary has asked her who she's going to ride with and all she ever does is shake her head and say she don't know."

At last the day arrived! Early that morning Gracie and I had an inspiration. We, too, would have a list for Canary. We appointed ourselves as a decorating committee. I got out my school pad and we went up and down the streets asking people to decorate their houses with flags for Canary's homecoming. Everyone agreed and we wrote their names down on our list.

Soon the town blossomed with red, white, and blue. Mr. Blankenbarger got out his Fourth of July bunting and draped it over his store windows. Even Ferd Fuchre stuck a flag on top of his barber pole.

Mrs. Overstreet went into Springfield on the morning train. Shortly after that Mrs. Antha and Uncle Will left in the big surrey. Mrs. Antha was carrying two bed pillows which she put on the back seat.

Canary wasn't to be discharged from the hospital until shortly after noon. But the Joneses left early so they could give their horses a rest before starting back. During this period they were going to eat dinner at the Leland Hotel. It was generally agreed they wouldn't run into Minnie Overstreet at the hotel for, despite the fact that she was going to rent the horseless carriage, she wasn't as free a spender as the Joneses.

"Oh dear," Mama said as we sat at dinner. "They'll both appear at the hospital at the same time and probably have an awful fight. Poor Canary! I wonder what she'll do?"

"Canary has as much dignity as anyone I know. Somehow she'll carry it off," Papa said.

"I'm not going to have an easy minute until I see her safely back in Tory," Mama said. "I can't settle down to anything. I'm going to sit out in the hammock all afternoon and wait to see what happens."

This seemed to be the attitude up Main Street and down Elm. As the afternoon wore away the porches were full of people. Relatives drove in from the country. Some of them brought picnic lunches. Canary's homecoming had turned an ordinary Thursday into a village holiday. Gracie came down to our house and brought her sewing. We were both making cross-stitched porch pillow covers. Gracie's was blue and white checked gingham and mine was red to match our hammock. On each colored square we placed a white cross. Miss Rose had showed us how to make them.

"If we get stuck, we can go over and ask Miss Rose," Gracie said. "She and her mother are on the Joneses' front porch."

"Mrs. Antha said she'd asked them," I explained. "They couldn't see a thing from where they live on the side street."

"Mrs. Huddleston and Brother Wilbur are coming down here. Mama asked them. I think they're going to bring ice, anyway Mama's made a lot of tea," I said.

In a few minutes Mrs. Huddleston and Wilbur arrived. He was pushing a wheelbarrow with a chunk of ice in it. Gracie and I went with him while he washed off the sawdust under the pump. Then he took a heavy ice pick out of his pocket and broke off a piece of ice for the bucket of tea which stood on the kitchen table. The rest was in an icebox Mama had made from a wooden box and lined with layers of paper that she'd tacked in. Into this we put all the bottles of root beer

190

we had. After finding out how much we enjoyed it, the patient who sent the first batch gave us a dozen more bottles.

"If you see any children who look hot and would like some root beer," Mama suggested, "you can ask them in for a cool drink."

"Oh, no," I said. "We want to play with Wilbur."

"And Mrs. Huddleston and I want to talk pickles," Mama said.

"I brought down the recipes you asked me for." Mrs. Huddleston opened her black leather bag and took out some folded papers. She had on the black voile again today. After dinner Mama had changed into her white dress with the lace up and down the seams. They made a contrast as they sat in the two porch rockers, the dark little woman in dead black and Mama, the beautiful blonde, in snowy white.

"You are so good to give these up for Antha and me to use for the pickles she's going to enter for the fair. It doesn't come off until October, but Antha simply has to win especially if Canary should decide to come home in the automobile," Mama said.

"Do you think she'd be that foolish?" Mrs. Huddleston asked.

"Gosh, I'd give my eye teeth, I mean my false teeth, to ride in one of those new-fangled contraptions," Wilbur said.

"You never will," Mrs. Huddleston said firmly. "None

of us will. I've seen notions come and go like that in my lifetime."

"Suppose we take our bicycles out and ride down the road and meet them," Gracie suggested. "Wilbur could borrow Mrs. Bradford's."

"No," Mrs. Huddleston said. "I wouldn't want Wilbur out on the road with one of those horseless carriages cavorting around."

We all knew how much Mrs. Huddleston loved Wilbur so nothing more was said, except Mama added, "I'll need you girls to help me pass the iced tea later on."

Then I led the way to the big elm by the porch while Wilbur and Gracie followed. We sat down on the rather sparse grass under the tree to talk.

"I wish you could invent something to make people make up their minds the right way," I suggested to Wilbur. "Then Canary would ride home with the Joneses."

"Nope," Wilbur answered, "that wouldn't be scientific."

"Could you invent a telescope that would look into the future?" Gracie asked. "If you could we would have known which one Canary was coming home with."

"That kinda sounds like God," Wilbur said. "But secret, strictly secret, I have thought about inventing a telescope, a big one that could look back of the stars."

"But do stars have backs? I thought they were round like an orange, just like the earth." Since one of my first teachers had explained the earth was an orange,

192

the thought had fascinated me. I liked to imagine it was juicy inside and that someday a very good farmer, who plowed deep, would hit the skin. Maybe that was what made the sun an orange color at times. Good farmers had scooped all the dirt off it.

"Don't be silly, Helene," Gracie said. "Everything has a back. Anyway, back of the stars is heaven."

"Maybe so," Wilbur agreed.

"Let's play our game about what we expect to find in heaven," I suggested.

"You girlies start," Wilbur said.

We went into our usual routine of golden streets, pearl rocking chairs, tumblers cut out of big diamonds, trees with emerald leaves, dishes set with rubies.

"And horseless carriages running around common," Wilbur added wistfully.

Around three o'clock we saw a great cloud of dust coming down the road. It was the automobile approaching. We all ran to the curbing.

"Stand back," Mama cautioned us.

"I'll get the flags," Gracie said running to a corner of the porch where we had a small stack to use for waving.

At last the car came in sight. It was an open car. In the front sat the driver wearing a dust coat, a cap, and goggles. Minnie Overstreet sat in the back. She, too, had on a duster, a cap, and a veil tied over her face. But she was alone.

"Oh poor Minnie!" Mama cried.

"But you wanted Mrs. Antha and Uncle Will to win," I said.

"I wanted them both to win," Mama answered.

"I bet that thing was going ten miles an hour," Wilbur said.

"Minnie's father would turn over in his grave if he'd see her doing a thing like this," Mrs. Huddleston said. "I bet this has cost her a pretty penny."

"Let's go down to her house," Gracie said.

"No," Mama said. "The kind thing is to leave her alone."

After that, various people who had been standing by her house drifted down to our neighborhood to stand near the Joneses' and watch them bring home Canary. From their conversation, we learned that no one had dared ask Minnie a thing. She got out of the car without speaking to anyone, walked into her house and closed the door. Then the automobile had left town, still going east up toward Taylorville. Maybe Minnie had arranged it that way so that no one would stop the driver on the way back and ask questions.

In about forty-five minutes, we could see more dust. It must be the Joneses' team and surrey coming. By this time, a great crowd had gathered in front of their house.

As they came into the village, Uncle Will slowed the horses to a walk. As they approached we could

194

see there was no one in the back seat. Where *was* Canary? We all hurried over to stand in the crowd by their driveway.

"I do hope Canary hasn't had a relapse," Mama said.

As they turned in, Uncle Will slowed the horses, and announced in a loud voice so that everyone could hear, "Canary wasn't at the hospital. Nobody knows where she's gone. The sisters said she just left before noon when the nurse on her section wasn't on duty."

"Maybe she had people in Springfield," Mrs. Huddleston said.

"Frank and I asked her that," Mama suggested, "and she said no. We asked her if she wanted to call in anybody before she was operated on."

"Where could she be?" "What's happened?" "Do you suppose she died and they hid her body?" Everybody was talking at once.

"Antha and I went all over town looking for her. And I guess Minnie did, too. We didn't pass anybody bringing her out on the road," Uncle Will said.

"It's as odd as a three dollar bill," Mrs. Antha said. "And the town looks so pretty with the flags and everything. But I tell you what. I just stirred up five gallons of ice cream this morning. I left Spider turning the crank. He don't make it as smooth as Will does, but if anybody would like to come round in the back yard we'll open it and everybody can have a dish of cream."

195

Quite a few people followed the team down the drive, including Gracie, Wilbur, and I.

In about half an hour Gracie, Wilbur, and I were still in the Joneses' yard having second dishes of ice cream when we heard another shout. We all ran to the front yard. Down the road came Canary on foot! Over her shoulder was a bulging pillowcase. In it I thought I could make out the outline of my perfume wheelbarrow. She turned in at our gate. We all ran over there.

"Here, Canary, sit down," Mama said. "What happened?"

"Nothing," said Canary.

"How did you get here?" Mrs. Huddleston asked.

"Walked," Canary answered.

"But why?" Mama asked with an edge to her voice.

"To get here," Canary answered.

By this time Papa came into the yard. Even if it had been a big homecoming holiday, he had been obliged to go into the country to make his round of calls. He took hold of Canary's hand and felt her pulse. "You seem all right."

"I'm all right," Canary said.

"We decorated everything for you," I said.

"Flags and everything for you," Gracie added.

"It was good and praise the Lord I'm here," Canary said. She'd been leaning back in her chair, then she sat up and made the longest speech I ever heard her

196

give. "It was this way. When I heard tell of how Mrs. Overstreet and Mrs. Jones were both wanting to bring me home, I didn't want to disappoint any of them or put anybody out so I just decided to walk home."

"But you *walked* those seven miles!" Papa said.

"Well, Doctor, I've always walked the country roads and toted things. Always walked barefooted. All us colored folks do down in Tennessee. I didn't have a sack so I just borrowed a pillowcase from the hospital. Folks brought me such pretty presents, I wanted to bring them home." She reached in the sack and pulled out a glass of jelly and a pink silk combing jacket. "Things like this. I'll wash the pillowcase and send it back to the hospital. And — " she looked up at Mama — "I worried a lot how you'd get your washing done while I was sick."

"A kind friend did it," Mama said.

"One of their patients," Gracie volunteered.

"Guess I'll go home now." Canary started to get up.

"Oh, no, stay here and rest," Mama said. "I'd planned to have you stay here in the guest room for a few days."

"Will's gone back to get you a nice dish of ice cream," Mrs. Antha said.

"No, thank you," Canary said. "I want to go home. I wanted to do that the most of anything. All the time I was in the hospital," she added.

"She should do just what she wants to do," Mrs. Antha said.

197

"We must have passed you on the road." Uncle Will stood there with a bowl of ice cream in his hand.

"Um hum," Canary answered. "I just hid behind some bushes. So as not to make hard feelings."

"I'll drive you over, Canary," Papa said. "Old Mike's hitched out in front. I'm going to insist on that. I'm the doctor."

"All right," Canary agreed.

And so on the great Canary homecoming holiday, the two of them started alone to her little house. No crowds followed.

"And to think we didn't even put up a flag on her house," Gracie said.

"Home's awful sweet," Wilbur said. "It don't need any flags flying. I'll never forget the time I came home from my trip to Iowa."

"Why, Wilbur!" Mrs. Huddleston cried, looking pleased.

"It makes me ashamed I put up a fight to bring her home," Mrs. Antha said.

"Don't worry, Antha." Mama put her hand on Mrs. Antha's shoulder. "I know she was pleased. She made that one speech and she'll probably never make another, but I know the flags and everything really pleased her. She's someone to be proud of in the village."

When Mr. Fenton heard the story, he was delighted with it all. "I think Frank was right," he said. "We should erect a statue to her. But why am I saying we?

198

I don't belong in Tory. Of course I might walk seven miles to get here," he added looking at Mama.

"Do you think they will really put up a statue to Canary?" I asked.

"I doubt it," Mama said. "People never put up statues to the right person."

"Who should they put up a statue to?" I asked.

"The country doctor," Mama said.

"To Papa!" I cried. "How wonderful! He's always getting left out of things."

"What do you mean?" Mr. Fenton asked.

"Oh nothing," I answered trying to make my voice sound like the grown-ups when they said *nothing* and meant a lot.

FIFTEEN

SOME DAYS AFTER CANARY'S HOMECOMING,
Gracie rode down to our house in the late morning.
Her flowered silk sewing bag swung on a handle bar
of her bicycle. I had a bag just like it, only where
Gracie's was yellow mine was pink. Mrs. Antha had
donated them to the church bazaar that spring, having
hired them made by a dressmaker in Springfield. She
set the price of two dollars on each bag. No one had
been willing to pay that much so Mrs. Antha bought
them back and gave them to Gracie and me. The fact
that we had started to cross-stitch sofa pillows gave
her a good excuse.

Gracie and her mother had a big fight over her bag,
Mrs. Baldwin saying it was far too pretty for a child
to use and wanting it for herself. Gracie wouldn't give
it up. Finally, Mr. Baldwin settled the quarrel by
saying that Mrs. Antha had given the bag to Gracie,
Mrs. Antha was one of the main supporters of the
church, and if Gracie didn't keep the bag she would
be offended.

Mama didn't ask for my bag but she did suggest that

since it was so exquisite, I had better keep it wrapped in a towel. When Gracie arrived, I ran in and brought out my bag, still wrapped in a towel with the pillow cover inside. I spread the towel on my lap and we started cross-stitching.

"I'm dying to make a pillow cover with an Indian's head on it." Gracie stopped to thread her needle. "You buy them already stamped at Bressmer's in Springfield. They have beads on the headdress part, already sewed on. All you have to do is to embroider the face and the feathers. They're just beautiful. I saw one made up."

"I don't know whether Mama would let me have one," I answered. They did sound beautiful to me, too, but I knew how Mama hated calendars with bright pictures and she might not take to a beaded Indian for the parlor. "But I did read about pillow covers we could make when we get through these."

"What are they?" Gracie asked.

"They're made of organdy. Mama or Mrs. Antha would have scraps of that to give us. You embroider the top with daisies and the words, *Daisies Won't Tell.* Mama could draw all that on for us to embroider. Then you fill them with torn-up love letters."

"But we don't have any love letters to tear up," Gracie protested.

"We can write our own, can't we?"

"What would we say?" Gracie asked.

"Oh we could write, I love you, and get things out

of poems and Shakespeare. You know — *Parting is such sweet sorrow* and *O! that I were a glove upon that hand. That I might touch that cheek!* and — "

"Lines from our songs," said Gracie, and she began to sing: "Daisy, Daisy, Give me your answer true, I'm half crazy, All for the love of you."

"Yes. That's what I mean. Mama's got a poem written on a piece of paper, folded up in her sewing box. I think Mr. Fenton copied it off for her. We can use that. Mama'll think I'm just after some thread." In a moment I was back with the paper. I smoothed it out and read it.

> *Blue were her eyes as the fairy-flax,*
> *Her cheeks like the dawn of day,*
> *And her bosom white as the hawthorn buds,*
> *That ope in the month of May.*

"But we couldn't use the word bosom. If Papa would see that in my pillow, he'd gosh blame all over the place," Gracie protested.

"But it says on the paper it was written by Longfellow. We have him in school," I said.

"You can use it if you want to in your pillow, but you have to be awful moral when you belong to a minister's family. Mama says so." Gracie shook her head.

"I guess so." It was nicer to be Doc's little girl.

"We'll have to change our handwriting so everybody'll think boys wrote the letters," Gracie said.

"We can do that easily," I answered. "Let's start

202

getting our torn-up love letters together. I'm getting tired of doing this pillow top. I'll go and get two sheets of Mama's light blue writing paper. She'll let me have that much if I tell her it's a project."

"And Mama has pink," Gracie said. "I can get two sheets of that because she's gone."

"Gone?" I questioned.

"Papa thinks she went into Springfield on the morning train."

"Didn't she say anything about it?" I was curious.

"No," Gracie said. "I was out on an errand on my bike and Papa had walked to the post office for the mail when she left."

I had been trained not to ask personal questions, a teaching which I couldn't always remember, but today I sensed Gracie was a little touchy on this subject so I didn't say anything more.

Soon Gracie was back with two sheets of the pink paper and a pad of white from her father's study. I had brought out two empty candy boxes to hold the torn-up pieces. Mr. Fenton always brought down candy and we saved the beautiful boxes. We began writing in what we felt was a bold, masculine hand several lines of I love you. Then I copied the fairy-flax poem. Gracie had been shown a love letter by one of the older Sunday School girls which ended, "With oceans of love and a kiss on every wave." She put that down on her paper.

"I want something from Longfellow, too," Gracie said as she finished this, "something that isn't dirty."

"There's 'The Village Blacksmith,' " I answered. "Let's go through that and get you a line." We both had learned the piece so we mumbled through the words and finally decided that Gracie could use, *Thus at the flaming forge of life our fortunes must be wrought.*

"Does that make you think of your papa?" I asked. "He's a big, strong man."

"I know," Gracie answered, "but he never does anything but depend on the Lord. He doesn't wrought things."

"He might have to someday," I insisted.

"Do the church people say that?" Gracie asked quickly.

"Oh, no," I answered. "I just thought of it myself."

We worked on until we had all the colored sheets and some of the white ones turned into love letters. Then we carefully tore them into pieces so as not to destroy any tidbit of sentiment, for although our pillows were to state clearly that *Daisies Won't Tell,* we wanted our friends to be able to read these juicy fragments of affection. As we sat working on these scraps of love we fortunately didn't know the havoc that soon would be wrought by love — at least that's what Mrs. Baldwin called it.

Gracie stayed on for dinner and supper, too, since

204

her mother did not come home on the afternoon train. Mama sent us down to invite Mr. Baldwin to come to supper, too, but he refused, saying he had to work on a sermon. I thought this was strange, knowing how much Mr. Baldwin enjoyed being asked out for a meal.

The next morning Gracie came down early. Her face was blotchy with tears. "Mama's run away," she sobbed.

"Oh, no," Mama said.

"She didn't come back!" Gracie cried.

"She's just gone off for a little visit, I'm sure. Have you had breakfast?" Mama asked.

Gracie shook her head.

"You sit down at Helene's place and I'll fix you some scrambled eggs. Helene, you pour a glass of milk, cut some bread and get out the fresh peach jam. After you've had breakfast, you'll feel better. While you're eating, I'm going down to talk to your father."

When Mama came back, she didn't say anything about her talk with Mr. Baldwin. I guess Gracie knew there was nothing to tell so all she said to Mama was that she had a headache. Mama got out her pretty smelling salts bottle and told Gracie to lie down on the sofa. "Now don't make a racket, Helene," she warned me. "I'm going over to Antha's to return a pie pan."

Soon she was back to say that the Joneses were going to drive out to their north farm and take us with them. Mrs. Antha was packing a lunch, we would stop at Hickory Point Grove and picnic.

Gracie forgot her headache and jumped up. Mama wiped off her face with a damp washcloth, brushed her curls over her finger, suggested that I rebraid my hair. I wouldn't do it. Braids never looked pretty, anyway.

The braids looked even worse by the time we got back. We stopped at the parsonage to let Gracie out. I had a feeling she dreaded going into the house. "Poor little tyke," Mrs. Antha said. Uncle Will turned the horses around. He blew his nose.

As we pulled into the Joneses' yard, Mama came running over. "My, you stayed a long time! It was so good of you to take the girls out of town for the day," she said. "Now I want you to come over to my house for supper for a change. I have everything all ready and the table set."

Uncle Will whistled for Spider to come over and put up the horses, and we walked through the yard.

"Is the barber shop still closed?" Uncle Will asked.

"Yes," Mama answered.

"You mean Ferd Fuchre isn't in town?" I asked.

"He must have gone off to visit some of his relatives," Mama said.

"That's what the Baldwins say about Mrs. Baldwin,

206

except she hasn't any money to get out to Arkansas,"
I answered.

"Maybe she saved some money," Mama suggested,
"or they sent her some money."

"They haven't any to send." I was proud of the fact
that I could even keep track of how much money people's distant relatives had. "I think I should go over
and tell Gracie that Ferd is away, too, and probably
he and Mrs. Baldwin are on a trip together. Then they
won't worry about Mrs. Baldwin any more."

"No," Mama said decidedly. "You know nothing
about this. None of us do. If anyone asks you any
questions about the Baldwins, tell them you know
nothing."

"Frank isn't home yet," Mama said as we all walked
through the back door, "but we won't wait. And what
do you think? I couldn't sit still today so I made a lemon
jelly cake."

"Looks like the best medicine I know," Uncle Will
peeked into the pantry, "to have you girls bustling
around a kitchen when you get upset. I'm sure going
to enjoy it. Now take Ferd, he — "

"Will Jones!" Mrs. Antha frowned at him. "Looks
like you can't talk about anything except the weather
without putting your foot in it."

"I didn't say a thing," he protested.

"You were going to." Mrs. Antha walked into the
front room to take off her hat. She had some new hat-

pins shaped like tiny golf clubs she'd just bought in Springfield. "They're that new game."

"Golf," I said as she handed me the pins to admire.

"Helene," Uncle Will called, "let's you and me pump the water and fill the tumblers."

"It's ready," Mama said when this was done. "There's really nothing but some cold veal loaf. This will make two picnic meals for you today."

"Cold food's just right for a hot day, and you always fix everything so tasty." Mrs. Antha eyed the platter with the thin sliced meat, surrounded by halves of deviled eggs and rings of green mango peppers from the garden.

We were all having our second piece of lemon jelly cake when Papa arrived.

"Any news?" Mama asked.

"Bryan seems to be picking up but I think McKinley's going to win," Papa said.

Everybody laughed although I was sure, even if they were staunch Republicans, this wasn't what they wanted to hear.

"Did you have fun at Uncle Will's farm, honey?" Papa turned to me.

"Oh, yes," I answered. "Gracie and I played we were living in a story called 'A Day at Grandpa's Farm.'"

"I never heard that," Uncle Will said. "Why don't you tell us the story, Miss Susan Dusanberry?"

I told them about how their north farm made me

think of the story. The Sunday School papers were full of accounts like that. The Thorntons, who were the Joneses' tenants there, had every animal that any author could dream of: horses, cows, pigs, sheep; and also chickens, ducks, geese, and turkeys. In addition, there were pets — two dogs, fourteen cats, and a goat. They had the proper scenery, too, a walnut grove, a rolling meadow, a green pasture, a big barn, two corn cribs, a huge haystack, and even a brook for wading. The characters in the story were Mr. Thornton, who always walked over the place with Uncle Will, Mrs. Thornton, who made caraway cookies, and the six Thornton children.

When I'd told Gracie about the story that day, she kept taking out her handkerchief to wipe her eyes. The storybook setup didn't cheer her up at all. But the Joneses seemed to like it.

It was nice to be a child and be heard as well as seen, and I could be heard before the Joneses. When I was taken into Springfield to visit Aunt Fan, it was understood that my role was purely to be observed.

After the dishes were done, I could sense I was in the way. I knew they wanted to talk about Mrs. Baldwin and weren't going to do it before me. The only way I'd hear any of the discussion was to go to bed and then do a little eavesdropping, or eardropping as Mrs. Antha sometimes called it.

So even before Mrs. Antha told me that my eyes

were like burnt holes in a blanket, I excused myself,
saying I was very sleepy. Quickly I slid out of my
clothes, read a chapter in *David Harum,* a new book
Mr. Fenton had brought down for Papa, then blew
out the light. I made my prayer short and snappy
for since Mrs. Baldwin was sure that prayers didn't
deliver the goods, I didn't think it was necessary for
me to put in my two cents for her with the Lord. Anyway, I wanted to start a little snoring to make everyone think I was asleep.

"The poor thing must have adenoids," I heard Papa
say. I calmed down on the snores because adenoids
were something that had to be cut out.

For a while there was more talk about the farm and
the crops, then I heard Mama ask, "Did you find out
anything?"

"I think I have a clue," Papa answered. "It's about
Ferd. I think Effie went off with him. It seems too
much of a coincidence that they would both disappear
the same day."

"They say she has been meeting him evenings and
walking around with him," Uncle Will said.

"And he has gone up there when Mr. Baldwin has
been out of town. Helene told us. You know how nosy
she is," Mama said.

"It doesn't look like the preacher's wife ought to run
off with the barber," Mrs. Antha said. "I don't set myself up to be highfalutin but — "

210

"I know exactly what Antha means," Mama said. "It seems so unusually common — a barber! And she couldn't be in love with that man!"

"Women are funny!" I could hear Papa laugh.

"Yep, Doc," Uncle Will said. "I suppose the girls would think it was all right if she'd of run off with Sam Blankenbarger."

"Will Jones! How you do go on," Mrs. Antha said. "But I shouldn't set myself up as a judge. Nobody'd ever want to run off with me."

"Nobody but me," Uncle Will said.

"About your clue, Frank?" Mama asked.

"I asked around," Papa went on, "Ferd hadn't said anything about going away. He always talks a lot, so this looks suspicious. But this afternoon Wilbur Newlin came into my office. He'd heard the talk. It's pretty well around town."

"Too bad," Mama interrupted.

"You can't sneeze in Tory without somebody sending over some horehound drops," Uncle Will said.

"Yes," Papa agreed. "Wilbur said last week Ferd asked him about the Chautauqua over on the Illinois River."

"Wilbur and his sister did go over there last summer," Mrs. Antha said. "But go on."

"Wilbur said Ferd told him they were having gospel singers from the west over there this week and wanted church choirs, or any singers, to come over and make

211

up a chorus. He asked Wilbur about staying all night and Wilbur told him you rented tents."

"That's just where they are!" Mrs. Antha cried.

"That's what I feel but isn't that the damnedest place for them to be?" Papa said. "After all, the Chautauqua is run by a church group."

I couldn't see anything wrong with that. Mr. Baldwin was a minister. No wonder Mrs. Baldwin went off to a church choir place. I hoped they'd win a prize. Mrs. Baldwin always wanted pretty things. As I thought it over I lost some of the conversation but I did catch on to the fact that Papa and Mr. Baldwin were going over to the Chautauqua tomorrow to see if they could find Mrs. Baldwin and Ferd, and Gracie was coming down to our house.

The next morning, Mr. Baldwin went into Springfield on the morning train. Papa drove in because he wanted to stop and see a patient on the way. From Springfield they were going to take an excursion train which ran daily over to the Chautauqua. This much I heard discussed. But I was warned not to mention that Papa and Mr. Baldwin had gone to the Chautauqua, in fact I was not to discuss Mrs. Baldwin in any way. From the unusual amount of callers Mama had I knew that curiosity was about to boil over. Everyone seemed scandalized. I came into our front room early that morning just in time to hear Miss Rose ask Mama if she wouldn't kneel in prayer and ask the Lord to save their pastor's wife's soul. Backing out hurriedly, so as not to embarrass Mama, I ran around the house and peeked in the window to see if Mama would consent. I was sure she wouldn't but felt better when I heard her refuse, definitely.

I knew why everyone was so stirred up. Mrs. Baldwin was too old to run away, only bad boys ran away, and when she had done such a thing she shouldn't have gone with Ferd because he was a sissy.

Later when I asked Papa about this he said, "You were right, honey. Never run off with a tenor."

Gracie stayed with us all day. At noon Mama went with us and we rode our bicycles out to Crow's Landing and picnicked. When we got home there was a note in the door from Mrs. Huddleston asking Gracie and me to come up to their house, help Wilbur with his inventions, and have supper with them. "Everyone is so kind," Mama commented as she handed the paper to me.

It was getting dark when Wilbur brought us home. "Let's sit out under the arbor in the back. You girls can chase fireflies," Mama suggested. We had just started this when we heard old Mike turn into the drive.

"It's Papa," I cried.

Gracie stood still. She had thought so many times that her mother would come in on the afternoon train or the evening train that I am sure she was afraid to ask again if she had been found.

213

"Your father and mother are at home, Gracie," Papa called when he saw us.

Gracie still didn't speak for a minute, then she started to run.

"Your bicycle is here," I called after her but she didn't seem to hear me.

"Don't go after her," Mama cautioned me. "She'll be down tomorrow after it."

We walked into the house. "I'm tired, dog tired," Papa said, throwing himself on the sofa. This was the first time I'd ever heard him complain.

"It was bad, wasn't it?" Mama said.

"If I could indulge myself by having a doctor I think I'd have a migraine." Papa put his hand on his temple.

"I'll make you some tea," Mama said.

"Good, that's what I always prescribe."

Mama was back in a few minutes with a cup of hot tea. Papa sat up and sipped it slowly.

"Was she at the Chautauqua?" Mama asked.

"Yes, and he was, too. In a tent registered as Mr. and Mrs. Will Jones."

"How dumb to take that name," Mama said.

"You mean they were pretending to be Mrs. Antha and Uncle Will?" I asked. "They must like the Joneses a lot to play that."

"It's a common name," Papa said. "We brought her back to Springfield and then drove out here."

214

"Did Ferd come with you?" I asked.

"Hell, no. I told that God-damned bastard never to set foot in Tory again. He's promised he won't. He says he knows a barber who wants the shop." Papa turned to me, "But look here, Helene, you stop asking questions."

"And don't repeat any of this," Mama said.

"You know, honey," Papa said to me, "Gracie's your best friend. George Baldwin says we are his best friends. I'm his doctor. Doctors always know lots of secrets. Living here with the doctor you're bound to find them out. Not telling these secrets is called professional ethics. Your mother always co-operates in this. I never have to say to her, don't tell. Do you think you can grow up right now — and be a real part of a doctor's family?"

"Yes." I crossed my heart. If I'd said anything more I would have cried. But I remembered with pride that I'd never told anyone about Mr. Fenton stealing Mrs. Antha's pink angel food. This had proved to me that I could keep secrets.

"That's fine. I knew you'd understand." From then on he talked to Mama. "George is very angry. He didn't speak all the way home. Effie cried some. She said she was swept off her feet, not too hard for she's pretty light-headed. George told me on the way over that she'd had few advantages. She was singing at a revival meeting where he was preaching when he met

215

her, and was a waitress in a depot restaurant. I imagine she felt when they got this church in Tory that she would be something in the community and would be willing to give up what she calls the fellows. I know this is a little hard for you to understand, Kate?"

"No," Mama hesitated. "She is pretty."

"Pretty?" Papa's tone was scornful. "But I guess I'm spoiled having you to look at every day."

"You spoil me. And — Effie never has any fun," Mama added.

"You mean they don't play hide and seek the way we do?" I was thinking how Mama and I would always giggle and give ourselves away when we found hard places to hide from Papa.

"Something like that," Mama agreed.

The next morning Gracie came down to our house. She had on the same blue dotted dress she had worn ever since the day her mother left, her hair wasn't brushed and I could tell she had been crying. In her hand she carried the box with the torn-up pieces of her love letters.

"I want to keep this down here," Gracie said. "Papa's awfully mad about love. I don't want him to find this stuff."

"What do you mean?" I asked.

"Last night I could hear him screaming at Mama, 'You call that love, don't mention love to me ever again.

216

I should have left you in that restaurant where I found you!' Oh Helene, you wouldn't believe the things he said. And then — then he did something just awful," Gracie lowered her voice.

"What?" I asked.

She couldn't even look at me.

"He burned up all Mama's clothes, every stitch! The ones she wore when she ran away, even her shoes. He started a fire in the cook stove and burned them up in there. I was awfully scared," she said.

I was too stunned to speak. At last I said, "Why?"

"I guess it was a punishment. Now Mama hasn't any white shoes to finish out the summer. She'll have to wear her high button blacks, and it was her pretty light blue dress."

"The one the beads went with?" I asked, remembering how we had been given the beads at the hoarfrost house.

"He burned up the beads, too." Gracie gulped. "And they were really mine."

"What did your mama do?" I asked.

"She cried and took on. She was crying again this morning. That's why I came down here," Gracie said. "I'm scared."

"Oh, I wouldn't be scared," I tried to think up something comforting. "Your father's a minister. He can't do anything very wrong. He was just real mad last night." Inside, I didn't believe this. There must be some

217

very good reason for his burning up the clothes when he knew that his family had such a hard time getting along. I remembered how mean people had been to poor Miss Rose when she burned up the feathers. It was awful to burn up good things! But I was going to practice professional ethics and not tell that Mr. Baldwin had burned up his wife's clothing, though I knew the story would leak out somehow. Everything did in Tory.

"Do you remember that line you copied off for your pillow, *Thus at the flaming forge of life our fortunes must be wrought?*" I asked. "Do you suppose your father was trying to do something like that?"

"I hate Longfellow." Gracie put her head down in the hammock and sobbed aloud. "I don't ever want to hear about burning in hell or burning anything."

Uncle Will must have been coming along the street and seen us for he came into the yard and stopped. "What's the matter with Gracie?" he asked.

"She *hates* Longfellow," I said.

"Poor little tyke," Uncle Will answered.

SIXTEEN

As mama had said, the summer of 1900 was like a meadowful of daisies, the more you picked, the more grew in their places.

Papa was the only one who'd hardly had time to walk in the meadow, let alone pick any flowers. I felt sad. After all, Papa had been the only person to see how thrilling the twentieth century was going to be. Just for predicting it, he should have got his share. As it was, he still made as many calls late at night. And he still got paid in potatoes and sausages. If only, just once, somebody would pay him with an Arabian horse or a fruit farm hung with ruby apples and emerald leaves.

Fortunately for Mrs. Baldwin, Mama had been right about the meadowful of daisies. The Toryites had picked her scrubby little adventure but they had let it wilt and had thrown it away so new daisies could grow. Their loyalty to our Tory pastor was bigger than their desire for a gaudy bouquet. Everyone still went to church despite the threats that Mr. Baldwin would be preaching to empty pews. The burning of his wife's

clothing seemed to have given Mr. Baldwin a new
standing as a man, something I couldn't understand.
Even the women of the village who were most noted
for their Bible-reading nodded to Mrs. Baldwin when
they passed her on the street.

It was funny, I thought. If Ferd Fuchre had been
like Mr. Fenton, none of this would have happened.
Mr. Fenton came to see us all, instead of meeting Mama
secretly. It had got so that Papa nearly always had to
be away when Mr. Fenton was there. Either somebody
was awfully sick or he had to drive into Springfield for
a consultation. I never knew him to make so many
evening calls. But Mr. Fenton and Ferd were as different as Newport and Tory so nobody ever talked about
my mother. And Mrs. Blankenbarger wouldn't have
made two gingham dresses for me, the way she did
for Gracie, so she'd have something new to wear to
school.

"I guess she's thanking her lucky stars this didn't
happen to Sam Blankenbarger," Uncle Will had said
when he'd heard of Mrs. Blankenbarger's gift. I didn't
understand this, but I could tell by the way Mrs. Antha
frowned, it was another one of those things Uncle Will
shouldn't have said.

Canary had recovered from her operation, was doing our washing again, and was busy watering her
orris, cooling it from the heat of the early September
sun. Mrs. Blankenbarger still had palsy of the stomach

and came each week to Papa's office for medicine, but she had no more almost-fatal attacks. Miss Rose had a beau! A Bible salesman! I thought it was an example of what Miss Rose taught us in Sunday School, the meek would inherit the earth.

Mrs. Antha had found a bottle of blue coloring fluid at a confectionery in Springfield that was made for candy and cake icing. It turned out to be fine for tinting cabbage, so the success of the red, white, and blue pickles was now assured. As Mrs. Antha said, the judge at the fair could eat the whole jar and he wouldn't have anything but an upset stomach. Each week Mrs. Antha and Mama thought up at least one new kind of pickle. Many of these were made and stored in the Joneses' fruit closet and there were still two weeks to go before the fair. We were certain Mrs. Antha would win the first prize.

Minnie Overstreet was busy, too, making pickles, but since we were sure she hadn't thought up any new varieties, she was not considered a threat. She had achieved a certain fame by bringing the first automobile to Tory. But in the feud over the gilded urn and the iron deer, Mrs. Antha felt she had come out on top for although Minnie Overstreet carried buckets of water, the flowers in the gilded urn looked droopy. "The deer sure stands the heat," Mrs. Antha often said.

In the back of the hardware store, Mr. Blankenbarger was making a dinner pail taller than a man. When it was done, it was to be lettered with the words: FOUR MORE YEARS OF THE FULL DINNER PAIL. This huge object was to be put on a hayrack and driven into Springfield as Tory's entry in the first Republican torchlight parade. Mr. Blankenbarger had sent away for the tin to make the huge pail and Brother Wilbur was helping solder it together.

The task had cheered Wilbur. He had been blue off and on since Maud S. had died. Maud S. was a race horse, almost twenty-six years old. Wilbur had a picture of her in his inventing shed and always referred to her lovingly as *Queen of the Track*. It had been his dream to see her, and now she was gone. Wilbur loved horse racing. Many times Gracie and I had crossed our hearts and hoped to die as we had promised not to repeat the stories he told us of his going to the races.

Mama's tramp, who usually came to see her in October on his way to Florida, appeared one morning in late August. He had decided to go to Hawaii, the new U. S. territory. He said he thought Mama needed shells from the Pacific Ocean as well as the Atlantic.

"He's just saying that," Mama told me after he had left. "He's bored with his routine. He's free to go anyplace, free as a bird. Not that birds are so free — they always go to exactly the same spots both summer and winter. After this I'm always going to say 'free as a tramp.'"

It *had* been an unusual summer: Mr. Fenton had

come to Tory with Harry Simpson's body; he had brought me a party and stolen Mrs. Antha's cake; Mama and Gracie and I had been given bicycles; I had saved Mrs. Blankenbarger's life; Gracie and I had been to the hoarfrost house in Springfield; deer and urns had blossomed on Tory front yards; Mrs. Baldwin and Ferd Fuchre, who weren't even second cousins, had gone to the Chautauqua together and stayed all night in the same tent; and I had committed myself, in front of Gracie and Mr. Blankenbarger, to getting a Don't Care soda at Dodd's drugstore someday. Perhaps these happenings weren't too strange since Papa had said that the new century would bring unaccountable wonders. I still worried about Papa, though. He said the twentieth century was going to bring the best of all possible worlds. So far as I was concerned, it *was* the best of all possible worlds. I hoped it would be for Papa, too.

With an electrifying new century before him, Papa had decided to turn over a new leaf, or rather a whole book of new leaves. On January 1, 1900, Papa started a scrapbook. He had always kept clippings about new ideas for farming against the day he would buy his fruit farm. Up to then, the clippings had been crowded untidily into a small desk drawer. Early in the summer he started to paste them neatly into his 1895 account book. He never sent out bills but kept accounts so when people came in to pay he could check off their debts. He knew if they hadn't settled up in five years it was just as well to cover up the figures. To these farming articles he planned to add items about events of local and national importance.

The first of these was dated January 3, 1900, and read: HAY COMPLETES NEGOTIATIONS FOR THE OPEN DOOR IN CHINA. Besides this, Papa wrote, *John Hay studied law in Springfield with his Uncle Milt.*

On the same page was an article from January 2 about the first autostage, an electric bus carrying twelve passengers which was running on Fifth Avenue in New York. Papa's comment, *Get a horse* was what everybody said in Tory.

Another January item described the opening of the Chicago Drainage Canal. Beside this Papa wrote, *Hope this won't hurt our catfish.* Below, dated July, was another comment, *Wint Fenton mixed up in litigation over this.* That must be another case that brought Mr. Fenton to Springfield, I decided.

On the next page, under an article on early spraying was a clipping of January 16 about the awarding of the contract for the first subway in New York. Underneath this Papa wrote, *Who'd want to be a damned mole?* Later he must have relented on this statement for with a blacker pencil he added, *Shouldn't be against progress in this new century.*

Further along, among items cut from *The Prairie Farmer* was pasted an article about Miss Olga Nethersole and her manager being arrested in New York for producing *Sappho*. This had really aroused Papa's wrath. *Oh hell*, he had written, and then added, *they say we are narrow-minded hicks out in the Middle West.*

In May, Papa had pasted a clipping about action being taken to make eight hours the legal number for working on government contracts. Papa's wistful comment on this was, *Lots of time for fishing.*

From then on, even if it were the beginning of a glorious new century, Papa lost interest. There was just one more entry, dated July 6, describing the nomination of William J. Bryan for the presidency and Adlai Ewing Stevenson for the vice-presidency. Papa, always a Republican, wrote beneath this, *Stevenson hails from Bloomington, Ill. I never did like Bloomington.*

I lay in the hammock and, for once, hoped Gracie wouldn't come to our house. If I was old enough to receive the strand of beads that Mr. Fenton had given me the week before, I was old enough to try to figure out what this summer meant. What, for instance, was Papa's scrapbook for? Was he like Mama in thinking that life was a lemon jelly cake? Was the scrapbook his way of escaping the Tory layer, his way of reaching out for the layers above? And Mr. Fenton? Was he a part of the lemon jelly cake? Once he had said Mama looked like the frosting on the cake to him. Maybe he'd been wrong. Maybe *he* was the icing.

I had hesitated in telling Mr. Fenton the silly thing about the summer being like a string of beads, but nevertheless I had. On his last visit, he had handed me a box from Marshall Field's store. In it was a strand of amber beads. There was a card engraved with his name, on which he had written, "It took a million years and an ocean to make these beads but it only took one summer to make me want to give them to you. They match your eyes."

It was my first grown-up compliment. I had been commended, but never before admired. When Uncle Will called me his Miss Susan Dusanberry, it was because he loved me and not because he thought I was a pretty little thing.

When Mr. Fenton had left, after giving me the beads, I had said to Mama, "You know how I told you that Mr. Fenton stepped right out of a book. Now I know which book. It's Grimm's, and he's our fairy godfather. Don't you think so?"

"Something like that," Mama had answered.

Now, as I lay looking at the deep September sky, I thought of Uncle Will and how he liked to say, "The sky's the limit." He was right. The sky probably was the limit to the things that could happen in the glorious new century, with a fairy godfather watching over Mama and Papa and me.

SEVENTEEN

IT WAS NOW THE THIRD WEEK IN SEPTEMBER. Papa and I were on the platform of the B. and O. station in Springfield. We had come to meet Mama. She had gone to Chicago to visit Mr. Fenton. At least that was what I had imagined. All Mama had said was that she was going off on a little trip.

When she told me she was going, I asked her if it were a shopping trip. Aunt Fan was always going up to the city to buy clothes and often begged Mama to go along.

"Do trips have to have adjectives? Couldn't it be just a trip?" Mama asked.

"If we had money you could go on shopping trips and buy ball dresses and cloth-topped shoes and pretty hats," I answered.

"I don't know where I'd wear ball dresses, since I live in my Tory layer of the lemon jelly cake," Mama said.

"But if Mr. Fenton were only our real fairy god-father, he might wave a wand and take us all out of that layer," I said.

227

"Did you think that up yourself?" Mama asked quickly.

"Yes," I answered. "Gracie says I'm silly the way I imagine things."

"I guess we're both silly. I imagine things, too," Mama said.

"You mean, like having a diamond tiara?" I asked.

"A diamond tiara would fall down over one ear. Sometimes even my hats do. No — " Mama hesitated — "I wasn't thinking of diamonds. I meant having a house with a cook and a parlormaid, and a carriage and a coachman, and sending you to finishing school, and — "

"Chocolate bonbons in silver dishes," I added.

"You're getting just like Mrs. Antha, always thinking of things to eat," Mama laughed. "She's wonderful. I love her. I don't know what I'd do without her."

"She isn't going to die, is she, even if she is fifty?" I was distressed.

"Oh, no," Mama assured me. "But about this trip. I've thought about it for some weeks and now I'm going. I must press my blue silk dress."

Mama got up. I could tell she wasn't going to say anything more about the trip. She had given me quite a talk a few days before about being curious. She had said no one who was well-bred asked personal questions. Somehow I sensed that if she had wanted me to know she was visiting Mr. Fenton, she would have told me; I could only imagine that was the reason.

Two days afterward, Mama left. I walked down to the morning train with her and then hurried to school, which had just opened and smelled of new plaster. "My mother's gone to Chicago on a trip," I announced proudly, as I stood with Gracie and the other little girls on our side of the schoolhouse.

"Why did she go?" Gracie asked.

"Oh, just because she wanted to," I answered. Then the bell rang.

But this wasn't the last of the questioning. By the next day everybody was asking me for details, not only the children, but women were stopping me on the street to find out all about Mama's trip. If I hadn't remembered that Papa had said I must always practice professional ethics, I might have made up some good stories about why Mama had gone away. I thought up several. One was that she was asked to go up and pose for an artist because she was so beautiful; another, that Mr. Fenton had just bought a beautiful yacht and wanted her to come up and take a ride.

But no. I really *was* going to practice professional ethics, so each time I answered in what I considered my best well-bred voice, "Mama's just gone off on a trip."

Gracie told me at recess on that second day that she had told her mother about Mama going to Chicago for just a little trip and Mrs. Baldwin had said, "Oh sure. She and the Virgin Mary." I had never thought

Mrs. Baldwin liked Mama. I had made up my mind it was because Mama was so much prettier. But now she was comparing her to Mary! She must love Mama.

That same afternoon, I went up to the church with Gracie to help pass refreshments at the missionary meeting. When I handed Mrs. Antha her coffee, she gave my skirt a yank in the back to pull it down over my petticoat which was supposed to be showing and announced in a loud voice. "Have to look after her. Her Mama's in Chicago seeing her grandpa. He had to be there on business."

"Why didn't you tell us that?" Mrs. Baldwin demanded of me.

"I don't know," I answered. And I didn't. It might be that Grandfather was in Chicago.

At supper that night, I told Papa about this. "That's just like Antha to have a good reason," he said. "But, by Jesus, your grandfather might be in Chicago. None of the Merriams, even your mother, are much on explaining their own business."

"Then is it professional ethics not to say anything about Grandfather being in Chicago?" I asked.

"Yes, in the most virulent form," Papa replied. "In other words, it's probably not true."

Each day Canary came to the house and cooked our meals and on the days she wasn't helping Mrs. Antha or some of the other women do their washing, she stayed all the time. Mama had made out lists of things to be done around the house, suggestions for meals and even for what hair ribbon of mine looked the best with which dress.

Mama was an excellent manager. She was always quick and efficient. I remembered the conversation Mama and Mr. Fenton had on his last visit, a week earlier. We had whisked through the dishes. It was afternoon. Mama was bathed, dressed, and scented with violet talcum powder. They were sitting under the grape arbor. I was perched in the apple tree reading *The Kentons,* a book Mr. Fenton had sent down to Mama. I hadn't cleaned up for the day, which was fortunate, for I had torn a rent in my black-ribbed morning stockings and honey was dripping down the front of my dress. Being true to the Mrs. Antha tradition that eating should accompany every act, I had taken a stack of crackers covered with honey up in the tree with me.

Mama had on her white dimity with a knot of blue ribbon at the neck. This had come on a dress Mrs. Antha had hired made. As soon as she saw it she decided it was too fancy-dancy for her, ripped it off and brought it over for Mama. The blue matched Mama's eyes and she looked beautiful as she sat there with the sunlight coming through the leaves and touching her hair. She was leaning back in her chair, her hands in her lap with her fingers locked together. Mr. Fenton sat in a chair by the table, drawing designs on an envelope he had taken from his pocket. Mama was talking and laughing. She was one of the few people who could laugh without sounding silly.

"I don't see how you manage drudgery gracefully," Mr. Fenton said. Here I stopped reading for I always liked to hear what Mr. Fenton said. It was even more fascinating to me than the conversation on the printed page.

"You mean that I'm capable?" Mama asked.

"I suppose so, but you don't look capable," Mr. Fenton answered.

"I expect you identify capability with glasses and hair drawn into a tight knot,'" Mama said.

"And a firm mouth," Mr. Fenton added. "But how do you do it? How do you live so prettily?"

"Prettily?"

"Yes," Mr. Fenton said. "Your house is always neat and orderly, and it has touches. I don't know just what they are but they are pretty. You move fast, but you don't rush and bustle. You're efficient, gosh-blamed efficient, to quote Mr. Baldwin. I know efficient isn't a pretty word to use in describing a woman."

"Pretty, too, seems to be your favorite word this afternoon," Mama laughed. "The only way I could answer these questions is to say that I have housework and cooking to do. The dishes wait for you in the sink, as they say here. There are no magic little people to wash them for you. And — "

"But even the soapsuds in your dishpan have rainbows in them," Mr. Fenton said.

"Now you are being poetic," Mama laughed again. "But, if I'm going to do all this housework, and I know that I am, I might as well do it as well as I can. You see, I was brought up on maxims, *a stitch in time saves nine; everything that is worth doing is worth doing well; order is heaven's first law* — my mother taught them to me. Oh, dear, I'm sounding like a prig, and stuffy, and — "

"No, go on." This time Mr. Fenton laughed.

"Of course I'm not always like this. I must have two sides to my nature. Sometimes I'm like my father. He hates drudgery. I don't know just how he made the money he did when he manufactured carriages."

"Business was an adventure to him. He was probably carried away with the great American dream of making money," Mr. Fenton suggested.

"I guess so. Right now he's terribly mad at William James. He used to like him. But yesterday I got a long letter from Father damning Mr. James's ideas of tying up practical consequences and values with philosophy," Mama said.

"In his next letter, your father'll be saying he likes James because James says he starts life afresh each morning," Mr. Fenton said.

"I suppose so," Mama agreed.

"Did you have an artist in your lineage?" Mr. Fenton asked.

"I don't know. Why?" Mama said.

"Who but you would think of painting this table under the arbor purple?" Mr. Fenton asked. "And putting a bowl of grape leaves in the center, with enough leaves in the bowl so the water shows and makes a spot of coolness."

"I just happened to think of purple. I mixed blue and red paint together to get the color. I always think the grapes look charming when they hang in great purple bunches in the fall, but the season is so short for them. This way I have purple here all summer. And anyway, I do have my practical side. When the grapes ripen and are purple, I can't let them hang too long. They'd go to waste. I pick them and make jelly. After I've done that this fall, I'll take some of Frank's labels, the ones he uses on pillboxes, write *Grape Jelly 1900* on them and paste them on the glasses. Oh, dear," Mama sighed. "Frank's always talking about the glorious new century. Sometimes I wonder if the record of my years will only be written on the labels of glasses of jelly and jams and cans of fruit."

"It would be damnable." Mr. Fenton reached over and touched Mama's hand. "You don't always have to stay in Tory."

"I suppose not." Mama's voice sank to a whisper.

* * *

234

Mr. Fenton was right. Mama was capable. She thought of details. I tightened the bow of the checked ribbon on my right braid. It was always slipping off because my hair was thinner on that side. Mama's list had specified blue-checked hair ribbon with dark blue chambray dress. I was wearing the blue dress and a thin little coat of navy blue serge made out of an old suit of Mama's. The wind had come up out of the southwest and was whipping around the corner of the station.

We had been walking up and down the platform ever since we arrived fifteen minutes before train time. On the drive into Springfield, Papa had talked very little. Usually he told me stories about the patients whose houses we passed on the way. Many times I had heard the story about Mr. Markwell, whom Papa almost lost, because when he told the family not to give him anything to drink except milk, the family had taken it so literally that he hadn't even had a drink of water. Papa had meant only to take him off whisky and coffee. But today Papa hadn't even said, "That's where that poor devil, Jim Markwell, lives."

Now, holding onto my straw sailor as we turned at the windy corner of the station, I asked, "Mama's surely going to come, isn't she?"

Papa stopped. "My God, you know — "

I was terrified. I felt in my pocket for my handkerchief.

235

"Don't cry, honey. Let's talk, instead. You know when Kate and I were first married, we used to come here to Chatterton's Opera House to see the plays. Kate always made me talk to her between the acts. She thought it looked so stupid to see couples who never spoke to each other. This isn't an intermission in a play, it's an intermission in our lives. So, by Jesus, let's talk."

"You still come in to plays." I wanted to help talk.

"Yes, but not enough. There's always some damned patient dying. I haven't taken Kate to enough plays, but what's even worse, I haven't provided enough drama in her life. And Tory is the kind of town that tends to eliminate the drama from life."

We kept on walking. "I've neglected your mother," Papa said. "I'm always gone. She's always alone."

"But you have to go out on calls," I said.

"I've probably gone when it wasn't necessary. I don't know why I felt it was important that I be on hand every time somebody took a dose of salts. I don't know why I had to be so God-damned dedicated to my profession. I've been a Christer, and I've laughed at other people who I thought were Christers."

"Mama says if you're going to stay alone a lot you must make yourself into somebody you enjoy for company. She told me that when Gracie couldn't come down last Friday. Mama's trying to do it herself."

"See? She's talked to you about being lonely." There was a pause. I didn't know what to answer. "Your

236

mother's a very smart woman — and very beautiful. Who was I to bury her in Tory? What was I thinking about? Why did I expect her to be married to the town just because I took it on for a wife? Everybody doesn't like the same kind of life."

Then we could see smoke and a light down the tracks. Papa took hold of my hand and held it tightly. Before this, meeting trains had been a high adventure, but now I trembled.

"It's going to be all right — I think," Papa said. The train pulled in and stopped with a grinding of wheels and a jerk.

Mama was standing in the vestibule.

I could see her brush off the soot and cinders from her coat with her hand. Back of her was Aunt Fan. Silas, Aunt Fan's coachman, came around from the back of the station. Everybody kissed everybody else while Silas gathered up the bags. Aunt Fan handed me a box. "Just some candy I brought you from Chicago," she explained.

Silas carried Mama's telescope with its worn straps and bulging sides over to where our horse was hitched. Aunt Fan walked along and waved as we left.

No one said anything. Mama put her arm around me and drew me close. "You've got a new hat." I broke the silence. "It's beautiful." It was a small round turban that tilted over one eye and had a red rose tucked in the veiling which swathed it.

237

"Do you like it?" Mama asked. "You should. It was awfully expensive. Fan and I saw it in a window. It cost six dollars and fifty cents. I had the money my father sent me for my birthday. I thought I could splurge."

"I didn't know Aunt Fan was going to be in Chicago with you," I said. "Was Grandfather there?"

"No! How did you get that idea?" Mama asked.

"I don't know," I mumbled. I wasn't going to tell on Mrs. Antha.

"I sent for Fan. I used some more of my money and sent her the telegram. I'd never sent a telegram before. I don't know why I didn't trust myself." I could see Mama was now talking to Papa. "I'd made up my mind about a lot of things on the way up. I looked out of the window. The country is really beautiful now with the corn in the shocks and — "

"The frost is on the pumpkin, don't forget that touch," Papa added.

I couldn't make out whether or not he was joking. Anyway, I didn't want to talk about pumpkins, so I asked, "Was Chicago wonderful?"

"Oh, yes!" Mama said. "We three had the best time. Wint took us to dinner at the Palmer House and another time to his downtown club. They all eat dinner at night up there. One day he got a carriage and we drove out to the Water Tower and saw the lake and lots of beautiful carriages on the boulevard. Then one night we went to a vaudeville show. Fan shopped. You know she has a modiste up there who makes all her clothes. We went to her shop for fittings."

"You should have your clothes made up there. If that dressmaker can make Fan look as well as she does, my God, what could she do for you!"

"I don't know," Mama said. "Don't think I want to spend my life in a tight corset like Fan does, especially since — well, since I've decided a lot of things about life."

"What, Kate?" Papa's voice trembled.

"I had a long time to think on the train going up. You know how it chugs, chugs, chugs along, the way you keep hitting the bottom of the bowl when you beat up a cake? Well, you know my lemon jelly cake theory and my feeling that I was in the Tory layer and — "

"Couldn't get out," I finished the sentence.

"I'm afraid I was silly enough to think that," Mama said. "I've been much too concerned with *layers* of the lemon jelly cake. No *layer* ever won a prize at the fair. It has to be the whole cake, or nothing at all."

"You mean Mrs. Antha couldn't win the pickle prize with just red pickles, or blue or white? It has to be all three?" I asked.

"Exactly. You must have known that, Frank. Your cake — your life — has always been big and beautiful and you've cut it in large wedges and shared it with

239

everybody. I want to do that, too, and enjoy it myself. You know I like sweets."

"Do you?" Papa asked.

Silas had helped Mama into the buggy first. She was sitting in the middle next to Papa. Now he gathered the reins in one hand, leaned over, took Mama in his arms and kissed her.

"I love you, Frank," Mama said in a low voice.

"Oh, Kate, Kate, my darling," he answered.

The horse slowed to a walk. Then Papa took the reins in both hands and said in a still shaky voice, "Get up, Mike."

"Do you know," he was talking to both of us now, "I don't think the horseless carriage is here to stay. How could you ever kiss your girl in one of those gas wagons?"

"Isn't Papa funny — and sweet?" Mama asked.

Mike's hoofs on the pavement beat out the answer, yes, yes, yes, yes.